*"Children are a gift from the Lord;
they are a reward from him."*

PSALM 127:3

CHAPTER ONE

Sunday, October 10, 1976

The room is dark like night. There are many unknowns in the dark. Those unknowns cause fear. I don't like fear. Right now, I feel as if fear is about to settle in right next to me, I flip the switch on the lamp.

Call out, "Mom."

There's no answer.

Call out again, "Mom, where are you?"

The thick silence in the tiny apartment is clear evidence I'm alone again. This scene is becoming my new normal. At eight-years-old I feel helpless. Much like the abandoned old man down the street. He looks tired. He looks weathered from living a life on the street. I utter stupid words my mother uses when she gets mad at me. It does me no good. I feel so alone in my heart right now, but even more on the outside.

Take a deep breath. Hands fidget. Kick off the dirty blanket. Wipe face over and over. Try to rid myself of stupid tears spilling down my cheeks. Hate my life. Have no dad. Mom comes and goes at all hours. She has no regard for my wellbeing.

Sometimes she tells me, "Henry, you're like the biggest mistake in my life. Why did I have you? Why?" The sadness seeps in. Leave the room. Close my eyes. Tears spill.

It's taken my heart a lifetime to break free of those painful words.

Take a deep breath. Hands fidget. Stare down at shadows on the wall. Count lines on floor. Stretch my body. Hang my head over to look at my broken shoes. They smell. Shoes have holes. Way too big for my little feet. Unlike the previous pair of shoes, these are good. I can walk to school with no blisters.

Tuck strands of hair so I can keep my eyes fixed on the door. Fear someone will bust the door open and take me. If that happens, I'm doomed. I'm eight-years-old. I'm clearly no match for anyone two times my size.

Take a deep breath. Hands Fidget. Have to calm down. Be brave. Brave is good. Being brave can help me.

Sitting on sofa I think of Tony. I wish I could be like him so badly. He lives across the street in a yellow house just behind a giant tree. He has a mom. The dad, he lives there too. He fixes everything. They live in the same house as Tony and his sister, Becky. How lucky is that? Sometimes I watch him and Becky play on the grass with their toys. See them too when they push each other on the swings. He eats small sausages with red sauce. Anytime the sun shines hot outside, Tony and his family take a trip in his dad's shiny convertible car. They return home when it gets dark. Laughing. Carrying shopping bags. They walk inside the house. I close the curtain.

Stupid tears are spilling again. Tears make me see blurry. Can't see the door. Can't see the door. Clean my face.

I'm tired of thinking about Tony and his great life. I need to think of my mom. My mom, I love her. With all my heart, I love her. She's all I have. Don't understand why she keeps failing me so miserably. Comes and goes whenever she wants. This afternoon, she walked out the door looking like she was going on one of her mysterious dates with the man in the red car.

I begged her to take me along.

"Can I go too?" I asked.

"No Henry, stay here." She said.

"I can put my shoes on."

She still said no.

"I promise I'll be good."

She pushed me out of the way.

"Can I stay with the neighbor, then?"

She made a face. "There is no money to pay the neighbor."

I cried out, "The dark scares me!"

She tells me, "You'll be fine."

"But please..." I cried.

"Henry, just stop. Listen to me. Lock the door, just like I showed you last time, and don't open it."

My desperation set in. "What time are you coming back?"

"In a few hours."

"How long is that?"

The door slammed shut.

In anger, I kicked the door with my broken shoes. Ran to the window. Pulled the curtain. Watched as the red car disappeared into traffic.

I think it's been more than a few hours now since my mom left. I know this because the birds outside the kitchen window are all gone. They go back to their hideaways when it gets dark. That's when I go to sleep too. Tonight I can't sleep. The rain is hitting the window. Cover my ears. Be brave. Be brave. Brave is good. Being brave can help me.

My emotions are running high. Fear doesn't leave me alone. I'm angry right now. Feel like I need to hit something. Look around the room. Walls are dirty white. Paint peeling off. Crayon drawings are everywhere. Should hit walls with my fists. Think fast. Could get hurt. Who will help me? Never mind. Punch cushions with my left hand. That's the hand I write with. Punch as hard as I can. Does me no good. Anger is still inside of me.

Where is she? Why is it taking her so long to return? How does she not understand I need her?

Move in circles around the tiny apartment. Count lines on floor again. Whispering into thin air. "I'm hungry. Mom, where are you? Mom, when are you coming back?" It's no use. Have to figure out life on my own for the moment.

Go back to sit on the sofa. Scratch my head. Not sure what to do next. I wait. Wait some more. Wait for as long as I can without shedding more tears. They come anyway. Mom tells me crying is for babies. Need to buckle up. Need to act like a big man. A big man doesn't cry. Doesn't show weakness.

I've taken those words and tucked them away deep somewhere in my heart. I've tried over the years to be a big man. Be a man with a face who doesn't show any emotion. Sometimes it works. Other times, not so much.

Pain suddenly hits the stomach. Pain feels like poking sticks. Curl up on the sofa. Squeeze stomach tightly. Maybe the pain will go away.

A while later pain is still there. Stomach needs food. Walk into the kitchen. It smells. Trash piled up in a corner. Trash in sink too. Cabinets are tall. Out of reach. I open the refrigerator instead. Bottles of mom's favorite drink are neatly stacked on top shelf. Something wrapped in mushy foil. Gross. Leave it alone. Small carton of milk sits on another shelf. Smells weird and looks crusty. Push it away. Tall cabinets are there again. Have to reach them. Push chair to counter. Other than a couple of dead roaches, there isn't much else except for open crackers. Strange color. Feel sticky. Waste no time. Savor each cracker. Take small bites. Chew crumbs in mouth over and over till they dissolve completely. No more pain. I'm ok now.

Take a deep breath. Hands Fidget. What to do next? Have no television like Tony. Sit on the floor next to the box. I keep belongings in the box. Scratch head. Look through the mess of stuff. Must find something to stay busy until mom returns.

Go fast cars. Wheels are broken. Push them aside.

Keep digging through a mess of stuff.

Pickup book. Pages marked with pencil scratches. Pages torn. Never mind. Shove it aside.

Don't give up. Must find something.

Find a red ball. It's small. Has good bounce.

Throw against the wall over and over. It's boring. Put it away.

Go back to sit on the sofa. Take a deep breath. Hands fidget. My mom is lost. Have to go find her. Eyes rest on the door again. Fear won't leave me alone. Can't open door.

Run to window. Pull curtain. Rain drops hitting window. Streetlight on the corner is casting shadows on cars. People are inside now. Love must be with them. Not here in this tiny apartment. Love doesn't live here.

Take a deep breath. Hands fidget. Must open door. Step outside. Find food. Find my mom. Take a deep breath. Open the door gently. Cold raindrops hit my face. Heart racing. Be brave. Be brave. Brave is good. Being brave can help me. My anxiety sets in. Hands fidget. Be brave. Be brave. The stairs. Where are they? Can't see them in the dark. Turn around. Go back. Knock on neighbor's door.

Door swings open, "Henry, what's wrong?"

"I'm hungry."

The lady pokes her head over my shoulder; she looks side to side. She says, "Where's your mother Henry? Did she leave you alone again?"

"She got stolen."

"I'm going to have to call the police."

"Do you have food?"

"Yes Henry. Come in. I'll get you something."

No time to waste. I quickly settled into a

chair at the table. Savor whatever food is being placed in front of me.

To calm my anxiety, the lady hands me a paper airplane. She begins her routine questioning.

"What time did your mom leave?"

"I don't know."

"Henry, did your mom tell you where she was going?"

"No."

"Who picked up your mom this time?"

"The man in the red car."

"Did your mom tell you what time she was coming back?"

"Few hours."

Lady grabs the phone. Dials zero. Conversation is swift. Gives me a sad look.

"Henry, when you finish eating, I'll take you back to your apartment."

"I have to find my mom."

"The police are coming in a few minutes. They can help you find your mom."

"Are they going to take me away, too?"

She looks at me with sad eyes and says, "I'm sorry, Henry."

CHAPTER TWO

*K*nock on door is loud. Cover my ears. Heart is racing. Is it mom?

Take a deep breath. Hands fidget. Open the door. No mom.

Man dressed in blue uniform. Mustache covers his mouth. He says, "I'm Officer Hernandez. You must be Henry Odin."

Fix my brown eyes on his face. "Are you going to take me to the place?" I ask.

"What place?"

"Place with all the kids."

"Have you been there before?"

I nod my head.

"Henry, you know you can't stay here by yourself."

My whimpering sounds are heard throughout the tiny apartment. Tears spill. I cry out, "I want my mom."

Officer clears his throat. Hugs me. Tells me, "I know, and I'm sorry you have to go through this."

Sadness seeps in.

Officer wipes his eyes. Pulls away. He is still talking, "Henry, go find you some clothes and a toy to take with you while I look around."

I make a face. Instead, I follow him around my tiny apartment as he takes notes. At one point, he stops in front of mom's dresser. Looks at the many photos scattered around. He picks up a couple of photos. Stashes them in his pocket. I return to sift through the mess of stuff. I have nothing good except my broken sneakers.

Officer looks at me, "Is that all you want to take?"

"My clothes are broken."

"What about a toy?"

"My toys are broken too."

Lady hugs me as I'm leaving with the officer.

She tells me, "Henry, I'm so sorry you have to go."

I push her away. "You didn't help me!" I cry out.

"It's better this way." She says.

I cry out again, "I want my mom."

She's still talking, "Henry, they are going to take good care of you."

Wipe teary eyes with the back of my hand. Follow the officer out the door to his car.

Pile into the back seat next to a small box of toys. Perfect distraction to get through this difficult moment. I sort through the box. There are many shiny toys. I pick out the best looking ones. Stuff them in my pockets.

Officer smiles at me through the rear-view mirror, "Henry you can have a toy from the box."

I respond, "Ok."

The police car pulls away from the only home I've ever known. Look away. Look away. My insides are broken. Am I ever going to see my mom again? Will I see Tony and Becky again? Will I see my life again?

Car ride is long. Car doesn't stop. Maybe we are going to look for my mom. All hope diminishes the moment the police car comes to a stop in front of a tall building. I see people walking through glass doors. At another entrance, there are two men dressed in blue pushing a long bed.

Pull away from the car window.

Take a deep breath. Hands fidget. I whimper, "I don't like coming here."

"No worries Henry, the visit here will not take long."

CHAPTER THREE

Lady behind the big window knows my story. They all know my story here.

She says, "Hello Officer Hernandez, a social worker is on her way."

Take a deep breath. Hands fidget. Count stripes on the wall. Noise too loud. Cover my ears.

Dressed in casual attire, Jackie Lozano rushes through the glass doors as quickly as she can. She greets the officer.

She's new. Knows nothing about me. Her green eyes are just like my mom's eyes. Smells like a pretty flower. Turns to look at me.

I step away. Hide behind officer.

She leans forward anyway. "Hi, you must be Henry."

I nod.

I flinch as she reaches to tuck the strands of hair spilling over my face. "Henry, you have beautiful brown eyes. How old are you?" She asks.

"I got eight."

"Mommy, leave you alone tonight?"

"She got stolen."

"I'm so sorry she got stolen. Where is your daddy?"

"I don't have one."

She puts her arms around me. Holds me. I never get hugs like that from my mom. In fact, I can't remember ever getting a hug from my mom.

Jackie speaks, "I'm so sorry, Henry."

She regains her pretty composure. "Henry, I know you have been here before, so we'll try to make this a fast visit."

"Doctor, check my tummy?" I ask.

"Yes, we have to make sure you are a healthy little boy."

"She didn't hurt me this time." I tell her.

Jackie chokes back the tears. "We can tell that to the doctor. Ok Henry, let's get you in the wagon so we can take a ride to see the doctor."

Take a deep breath. Hands fidget.

Officer waves as I disappear around the corner.

A short time later, I return with stickers and a red bendable toy. "Did you find my mom?" I ask the officer.

Officer clears his throat, "I'm sorry Henry, but we have to take you to the children's home."

"I don't like that place." Take a deep breath. Hands fidget. Count stripes on wall again.

Jackie interrupts, "Officer Hernandez, I can take Henry if you need to get back to your calls."

As hard as I can, I squeeze the officer's hand. I burst out in my loudest voice, "No, don't make me go with her! I don't like her!"

Officer motions to Jackie, "It's okay, I will take him."

Chapter Four

The drive leading up to the children's home is dark and scary. I think I was just here days ago, but I'm not sure. All my days are the same right now. I don't even know if tomorrow I will go to school or stay home. I press my head on the car window. Can't see the canopy of tall trees along the winding pebbled road tonight. Where did they go?

Take a deep breath. Hands fidget.

Officer turns to look at me, "What's wrong Henry?"

"Can't see trees. Where did they go?"

"Henry, it's ok. The trees are still here. We can't see them right now. They are hiding inside the cloud of rain."

"When am I going to see them again?"

"When the cloud of rain disappears tomorrow morning."

As we near the end of the road, I look for the bird fountain too. Can't see it. Rub my eyes. Lost inside the cloud of rain, too? I scoot to the other window. Why can't I see the bird fountain? Take a deep breath. Hands fidget.

"What's wrong now, Henry?"

"I can't see the bird fountain."

"Henry, it's inside the cloud of rain too. Tomorrow you'll be able to see it."

I shake my head. "Not the same place."

"Yes, it is Henry. You'll see. We are almost there."

Car finally stops. Can't see the house. It's hiding inside the cloud of rain.

Officer says to me, "You ready?"

I shake my head. Heart is racing. Turn to the window. Sadness seeps in. Try to hide my teary eyes. Can't believe I'm back at this place. I'm so tired of being shuffled around like a punched up doll with no voice box. Take a deep breath. Hands fidget.

In the rain, the officer leads me up the walkway. The front of the house looks weathered, front door as well. Rain makes everything look ugly. Shiny plaque by door catches my eye. Must be new. Has letters and numbers - PSALM 147:3. No idea what that is. I can't read too well.

Front door swings open, she steps out. She heads in my direction with an umbrella. Putting her arms around me, she tells me, "Henry, I am so happy to see you. Your hair is so long. Your patch of blond hair just keeps growing. Are you hungry?"

I nod.

"We have some delicious dinner waiting for you."

Officer cuts in, "The social worker was supposed to bring Henry, but he wouldn't come with her."

Lady smiles, "I'm Mary Ann Jones, the director of the children's home. It's ok. Henry has been here before."

She turns her attention back to me. "Come on Henry. Let's get you out of the rain and inside."

Mary Ann Jones. Pretty name. She is nice to me when I come here. Gives me toys. Gives me new clothes. Food here is always good too. Wish my mom could be more like her.

This place is like my second home. Everyone here knows my story too. They are nice but loud, like at school. Cover my ears. Heart racing.

"Look Henry, you get to share this room with Joseph and Billy. They are in the common room playing games. You'll get to meet them later. Your bed is by the corner. By the window are baskets with toys. Tomorrow you can play with them."

Take a deep breath. Hands fidget. Count squares on bed sheet. Don't like room. Room is too big. Looks like hospital room. Walls are grey. Ugly color. Makes me sad.

Mary Ann notes my anxiety. She puts her arm around me to comfort me. "What's wrong Henry? Are you feeling anxious?"

I nod.

"No worries Henry, everything is going to be just fine."

"I want to go back home."

Officer steps in to reason with me, "You can't stay there alone. We need to find your mom first. If we find her, you can go back home."

Mary Ann dismisses the officer to the side. Ushers me out of room. Leads me to dining hall. Of all the rooms in the house, this room is the one I like the most. The aroma of a well-cooked meal usually lingers around for hours. Scraps of old wood cover the walls. Ceiling skylights tower over the great room. Fireplace made of chipped stones is just the right size for Santa Claus to gather with his bag of presents. Maybe this time mom and I can come back for Christmas.

A lady holding two plates of food comes around to my table. Places them in front of me. I take in the aroma of delicious food. On one side of the big plate, there are mini sausages smothered in special red sauce. They are my favorite. They are Tony's favorite too. A slice of fresh baked bread with a generous spread of warm butter sits on the edge of the plate. Look over to the other side of the plate and what do I see? It's green beans. Do not care for them at all. Not only do they look ugly, but they smell and taste awful. Scoot them over to the edge. Better yet, just throw them on the floor instead. Looking every bit delicious is the big round cookie on the much smaller plate. Hold it in my hand for a moment, taking in the sweet scent of chocolate. To make it look pretty, I arrange it back on the plate. Have it later with my glass of cold milk.

Officer adjusts his shirt collar. A sign it is time for him to say goodbye. He clears his throat. Approaches the table and says, "Henry, I have to get back to work."

"Are you going to find my mom?" I ask.

"I will try my best."

"Tell my mom I'm here. Waiting for her to pick me up."

CHAPTER FIVE

Sunday, October 24, 1976 (Two weeks later)

"Henry, you like your new red shirt?" Mary Ann asked.

"When is my mom coming to get me? I want to go home."

"Oh Henry, I wish you could go home too, but Officer Hernandez hasn't found your mom yet."

Take a deep breath. Hands fidget. Count squares on bed sheet. "Am I going to live here forever?"

Mary Ann replies, "No Henry, we are looking for relatives."

"What's that?"

"Oh, like an aunt, uncle, or maybe even a grandma. One of them can provide a suitable home for you just until your mom comes back."

Take a deep breath. Hands fidget. "Are they going to hurt me?"

Mary Ann put her arm around me. It seems she, too, is finding it hard to keep from displaying tears. She tells me. "No one is going to hurt you."

"My mom hurts me."

"I'm so sorry, Henry. I'm praying for your life to get better."

Sadness seeps in, "Ok."

"Let's have some fun today. Come on Henry. Take my hand. We are going outside to the playground to find our other friends. We can also watch the fish swim in the pond. How about kickball? I know you like to kick the ball around. We can find a friend to play kickball with you, too."

"I want to take my toy."

"Of course."

As we approached the patio door, Officer Hernandez was coming around the corner. I ran as fast as I could to greet him. "Did you get my mom back?"

"Not yet, Henry, we are still trying." Officer Hernandez replied.

Mary Ann opened the patio door for me. "Henry, you go out and play. I need to talk to Officer Hernandez for a moment. And stay away from the dirt pile over by the tree."

"Ok."

"I think we may have found a relative." The officer announced to Mary Ann.

"What relative?"

"Seems Henry has a grandmother. She lives just outside the city."

"Have you talked to her yet?"

"I tried. She seems reluctant. Not interested in knowing anything about her daughter's disappearance. Guess there isn't much of a relationship there. I'm hoping you can try calling her. You might be better at explaining Henry's situation and in more detail."

"Oh yes, I can call her this afternoon. You and I know very well children that are placed with caring and loving relatives will have thriving lives. Oh, how I wish Henry could be in a suitable home. He comes and goes. I'm concerned about how life is going to turn out for him if this continues."

CHAPTER SIX

Mary Ann looked at the number scribbled on a piece of paper. She took a deep breath.

"Hello, can I speak to Jessa Odin?"

"Who is this?"

"My name is Mary Ann Jones. I'm calling from a children's home in the city. Are you Jessa Odin?"

"What do you want?"

"Are you Jessa Odin?"

Silence.

"Ms. Odin, are you there? Please, I need your help."

"Why are you calling?"

"Are you related to Liset Odin?"

"She's my daughter."

"Have you seen your daughter?"

"Did something happen?"

"Liset disappeared a couple of weeks ago. I'm trying to locate relatives of hers."

"I haven't heard from my daughter in years. No telling where she might be hiding. I don't care to know. Leave me alone."

"No, wait, please don't hang up. This isn't only about Liset. It's about the little boy."

"Boy? What boy?"

"Liset has a son. Social services transferred him here a couple of weeks ago."

Silence.

"Ms. Odin? Ms. Odin? Are you there?"

Was it possible this lady did not know Henry existed? Why would it even surprise Mary Ann? Many of these cases all seemed to have a common thread—relatives who never seemed to have any knowledge of the missing parent or the abandoned child. Sometimes they would even flat out lie to protect themselves.

"Ms. Odin, are you there?"

"Yes, I'm here."

"We think the little boy might be of some relation to you."

"How old is he?"

"Eight."

"His name?"

"Henry Odin."

"Odin? And the father?"

"There is no father listed on the paperwork. Looks like it's just him and Liset."

"No, I don't want to get involved."

"Ms. Odin, please, you might be all he has right now."

Silence.

"Ms. Odin?"

"Maybe I can come see him."

"Oh, that would be great, but I would need

for you to bring some proof identifying you are Liset's mother."

"Like what?"

"If you have photos, a birth certificate. Anything that might show us there's a relation between you and Liset."

"So, how is the boy?" Jessa asked.

"You know, for an eight-year-old who's been through this a few times; he is pretty strong on the outside. I'm sure, though, he is suffering on the inside."

Silence.

"Ms. Odin?"

"Yes, ok, I'll come see him."

"If you can get everything together by tomorrow, you can see him the following day."

"I'll see what I can do." Jessa replied.

CHAPTER SEVEN

M ary Ann felt relieved to pair Henry with a relative. She wanted to tell him the good news but feared he would not respond well, so she decided she would tell him later.

She approached the back patio door as Henry was coming back in.

"Henry, oh my goodness, you've been poking at the dirt pile again. What's wrong?"

"I'm sad."

"Oh, I know how you feel, little one."

Mary Ann took time out of her busy day to sit with me. She cradled me in her arms. Talked to me in her pretty voice, "It is difficult to be away from home for so long. Home is where you feel safe and comfortable. Home has all your favorite things. I'm so sorry this is happening to you. I hope Officer Hernandez can find your mom real soon so you can return home. For now though, we are happy you are here with us."

Anytime I look at Mary Ann's soft, pretty face, my anxiety fades away. She tucks strands of hair spilling over my face. A sign she cares about how I look. She wipes my teary eyes. I can hear the kindness in her pretty voice. Like today when she tells me, "Henry, you must not cry so much. I'm sure you will see your mom real soon. Let's try to pull out some happiness today. Go get cleaned up for lunch. Today, we are serving cheeseburgers and fries with a yummy chocolate treat."

For the first time in my life, I feel as if someone cares about me. I wish my mom could be more like Mary Ann.

Hours later, the kids were back out on the playground. Except for me. I went back to my room where it's quiet. Sometimes the noise on the playground gets too loud. I have to cover my ears.

A while later, Mary Ann noticed my absence on the playground. Came looking for me.

"Henry, what happened to playing outside with the rest of the kids?"

"It's too loud. Hurts my ears."

She looked at me most unusually. "Henry, do you have trouble with loud noises?"

"Sometimes."

"I'm going to get you some friendly headphones to help you with the loud noises."

"What's that?"

"It's something that covers your ears, so the noise isn't so loud and you can go out and play."

"Is it going to hurt me?"

"No Henry, the headphones will not hurt you. In fact, they might make you feel better."

"Can I stay in here?"

Mary Ann moved me to the window. She pointed to the playground. "Henry, every kid you see playing outside is feeling sad too, yet they are all attempting to find their happiness. Look, they are smiling, laughing and playing."

I raised my sad eyes to her. "Happiness?"

She smiled back at me, "Yes and you can pull out some of that happiness too. In fact, maybe by this afternoon."

I made a face.

She continued, "It's Sunday! You know what it means, don't you?"

I shrugged, pretended I didn't know what she was talking about.

She seemed determined to get me interested in the afternoon events. "The clowns come to put on their magic show. I think today they are bringing a pony too. It will be fun, you'll see."

At that moment, a slight glimmer appeared in my eyes. Feeling like everything was going to be ok. All thanks to Mary Ann and her caring spirit.

"Is that a bit of happiness I see in your eyes already?"

I cracked a slight smile.

CHAPTER EIGHT

Tuesday, October 26, 1976 (Two days later)

S unshine lit up the skies early morning. After breakfast was served, I soon found myself seated under the tree with the big branches. I picked up a few great poking sticks to play on the pile of dirt. A short time later, I witnessed a small bird flying in and out of the branches above and then landing on the ground. I couldn't help but wonder how something so small could bridge the sky with earth so well. This little creature had unlimited freedom to fly over the entire blue sky. It could also walk the entire earth and even have all the ocean water to swim whenever it wanted to. It was clearly the way to a happy life. I threw my sticks down. Took to climbing the tree. Maybe I could learn to fly like the bird too.

Mary Ann rushed over. "Henry, get down. You know you aren't supposed to climb the trees."

"I want to fly."

"Henry, why do you want to fly?"

"I want to be a bird."

"And why do you want to be a bird?"

"Can go all the places."

"You are very brave to want to fly."

"Find my mom. Go see Tony too."

"Officer Hernandez is still looking for your mom. Let's get you down. I have a surprise for you. I think this will make you happy."

"Is it my mom?"

"No, but remember I told you the other day, we were looking for your relatives?"

I looked at her, somewhat confused.

"Looks like you may have a grandma."

"Grandma?"

"Yes, Henry, Officer Hernandez found your grandma."

I shook my head. "No, I don't have one."

"Your mom may have said you don't have one because she lost touch with her."

"Is she going to hurt me, too?" Take a deep breath. Hands fidget. Count rocks.

Mary Ann put her arm around me. "Breathe Henry. Breathe one more time. Not to worry. We won't let anyone hurt you. Let's get you cleaned up so you can meet your grandma."

"When is she coming?"

"Later today."

Take a deep breath. Hands fidget. Keep counting rocks.

Two hours later.

Jessa Odin walked through the front door of the children's home, adjusting the thin red scarf around her neck. She looked thin and frail, giving the appearance of someone much older. Perhaps stemming from a long, hard life. She combed her fingers through her short gray hair as she waited in the lobby.

Mary Ann held out her soft hand. "Hello, are you Jessa Odin?"

"Where is he?"

"I'm Mary Ann Jones, the director. We spoke on the phone."

"Is he still here?"

"Yes."

"Well, where is he? I want to see him."

Mary Ann could sense the urgency in Jessa Odin's voice. "Please, before you see him, I need to review your documents and tell you a bit about Henry's situation."

"What more can you tell me? My daughter disappeared. The boy is stuck here with you until she returns. That's pretty much it. Isn't it? Or is there more?"

Mary Ann began, "Henry's mother, or rather Liset, your daughter has been in and out of jail over the last few years. Each time, he ends up here for a day or two. This time around, it's different. Seems Liset disappeared a couple of weeks ago, and no one can find her. Henry is in a very fragile state. He has anxiety issues and has some form of autism. Meaning he can function unless he gets stressed and there is a lot of commotion around. Therapist has taught him breathing techniques. Sometimes, when he feels overwhelmed, he will count things. It can be chairs, petals on a flower, even the tiles on the floor. Anything to help him calm down. He is sensitive to loud noises and when that happens, he covers his ears. He also likes his food separated on his plate, otherwise he won't eat."

"Oh no, poor little thing. So he has an illness?"

"No, it's not an illness. It's more like a disability. He could outgrow some of the symptoms someday. We don't know. Right now, he needs to be in a calm environment in order to feel safe and not feel so stressed."

"You mentioned the father is not around."

"From what we know, there is no father's name on the birth registry."

"Does Henry know about me?"

"I talked to him this morning. He's not accepting the idea of relatives right now. It's a common thing."

Jessa Odin stood up. "Maybe it was a mistake for me to come."

"Ms. Odin, wait. It's all going to work out. I've been doing this awhile. It is going to take change on your part and on Henry's part for all this to work."

Jessa Odin drew her eyebrows in. "What do you mean for this to work?"

"We will talk more later, but right now, Henry is waiting." Mary Ann went back to looking at the documents. "Everything appears to be in order, so if you are ready, I can take you to go meet Henry. Oh, and I would advise you to carefully choose your words. Do not make any promises you cannot keep."

CHAPTER NINE

M ary Ann came into the room to find me sitting on the floor while I was trying to make sense of all the amazing toys I had taken from the basket. To assess them correctly, I scattered them all around. I found cars, trucks of all sizes. The best part about playing with them was the wheels. They were all intact. None appeared to be broken.

She looked at me in her usual sweet demeanor. I couldn't help but wish my mom could be more like her. She tucked the strands of hair away from my face and said, "Henry, someone is here to see you."

I ran to the door, "Mom!"

"No Henry, not mom, your grandma. She is standing by the door."

I shouted, "No, no." Take a deep breath. Hands fidget. Heart racing. Count toys.

Mary Ann saw the fear in my eyes. "Henry, calm down. Take a deep breath. I'm not leaving your side. Staying right here with you. I promise."

She pulled the door open. Signaled for Jessa to come in.

The moment I saw Jessa Odin come through the door; I grabbed Mary Ann's hand and held on to it. Take a deep breath. Take a deep breath.

She looked nothing like mom except for her thin body. I hid behind Mary Ann. Be brave. Brave is good. Being brave can help me.

Upon seeing Henry, Jessa's heart took an unexpected turn. She tried to keep her emotions intact. He looked nothing like her daughter. He was small, skinny, a head full of messed up hair with a blond patch of something on the side. Perhaps he resembled the man who fathered him. She regained her composure, hoping she could connect with him. Her voice trembled as she spoke. "Hi Henry." Her wrinkled hands held out a small white box wrapped in a red bow. "This is for you." She said.

I didn't know what to make of it. I hesitated at first. This stranger I had never seen before was paying me a visit and gifting me something. Why?

Mary Ann encouraged me, "Henry, your grandma has brought you a gift."

I grabbed the gift from her hands and returned to Mary Ann's side.

Mary Ann put her arm around me. It was a sign everything was going to be ok.

My brown eyes looked up at Mary Ann.

"Henry it's ok, you can open the box."

I pulled on the bow. Opened the box to find four shiny cars, each in a unique style and color. I liked them. Tore open the wrappers and lined them up on the floor. Moving them back and forth. Making sure the wheels were intact and not broken.

Jessa moved closer. "Do you like them?"

I nodded.

For most of the forty-five minute visit, Jessa kept her composure intact. She seemed genuine in trying to connect with me. At moments, I too found some interest in engaging with her. A short time later, her visit ended. She hugged me. Whispered to me, "I pray God will protect you while you wait for your mom to return."

I lifted my broken eyes to her and asked, "Can I keep the toys?"

She smiled back. "Of course you can."

Jessa Odin didn't seem so bad. Her pleasant voice made me like her. Maybe she could help me find my mom. My heart eased up a bit. The door closed. I went back to playing with the new spiffy cars. It was the perfect distraction for any kid like me.

After the door shut behind them, Mary Ann asked Jessa, "Do you have a moment, Ms. Odin?"

Jessa rearranged her red scarf, trying to come up with an excuse to say no, but she couldn't come up with anything. She said, "Guess I do."

Mary Ann opened the patio door. "Lets walk out to the garden." She said.

Looking around the garden, trying to gather the right words before speaking, Mary Ann crossed her arms, sighed and then spoke. "A child's heart at this young age doesn't hold on to a record of wrongs. From the moment they are born, they only know to love, to trust, and to believe."

"What are you trying to say?"

"We don't know at this point when your daughter, Liset, will return. We strive hard to make this place a home as much as we can for the children who are being forced into this new life. You know, just by looking around this place, it lacks the warmth of a proper home. The longer they stay in isolation here; the harder it will be for them to return and adjust to the outside world. Distrust sets in. They may feel as if life is treating them unfairly, thus creating bitter hearts. Anytime that happens, the love they once knew disappears."

"What are you trying to tell me?"

Mary Ann continued, "It is hard for some of these children to live in an environment like this. There aren't enough adults who can spend quality time with every child. We do what we can by looking for relatives that can provide the child with a loving and secure environment."

Jessa wiped her teary eyes.

"With the support of loving relatives, these children do better in school, in life, in relationships."

Jessa took a seat on the bench. Placed her hands on her lap and stared out into the garden. "What do you want from me?" She asked.

"Ms. Odin, you appear to be the only relative Henry may have at the moment who can care for him."

"So what happens if my daughter returns and wants Henry back?"

"If she returns, favor would not be on her side because she abandoned her child. She would have to have a miracle reason for having left her eight-year-old son alone. We are now approaching the third week, and we still know nothing."

Jessa wiped her eyes again, "I don't know. I would need to think about it. I'm not young anymore. There are health issues. The income I live on is very limited. There isn't any extra money in my budget to raise a child, much less one with a disability."

"I understand your situation. We see many grandparents who are having similar challenges, but they make it work. Please, just think about it."

Chapter Ten

Wednesday, November 10, 1976
(One month later)

"When is my mom coming back? I want her to come get me."

Mary Ann sat down next to me. Looked around the room for a moment and then spoke, "We don't know how much longer your mom will be gone. Do you think you might like to go stay with your grandma while you wait for your mom to come back?"

I tried my best to ignore Mary Ann's words. My eyes scanned the room in every direction. Take a deep breath. Take a deep breath. I felt defeated without even as much as a word on my part. I was alone in all this. Mary Ann looked like she wanted to help me, yet it seemed like she was just hindering my situation. My eyes rested on Mary Ann's face again. She was still talking. Feeling like I'm so far away right now. Can't hear her words. Fear is setting in. As hard as I can, I am fighting back tears. Remembering my mom's words, "Only babies cry." I'm no baby. I try hard, yet the tears they come, anyway. Wipe my face with the back of my hand. My eyes scan the room again. Can't remember what day it is anymore. Miss my friend Tony, and my school. Missing the sofa where I sleep too. Just want my mom to come get me. She always comes back. Why is it taking her so long to come get me? Did I do something wrong? Is she mad at me? That's it. I did something wrong. And now she won't come get me. Take a deep breath. Hands fidget. Count squares on bed sheet.

"Henry, what's wrong?"

Take a deep breath. Take a deep breath. "I want my mom to come get me."

"I know you do. And I'm so sorry it's taking her so long to come get you."

"Can grandma take me to my house so we can wait for my mom?"

"You know, Henry, I think you might be more comfortable staying at your grandma's house right now. I went to visit her the other day. She has a pretty house. You can have your own room where you can play with all your new toys. There is even a backyard for you to run around and chase butterflies."

"Can she take me to get ice cream?"

Mary Ann said, "She told me there is an ice cream truck that drives by her house every day.

Think she would be happy to buy you an ice cream."

"Can she take me to see Tony?"

"Is he a friend from school?"

"He lives across the street."

"We will have to ask her."

I was growing tired of staring at the grey walls day and night and of not being able to see the world on the outside. Feeling alone in my heart. Take a deep breath. Take a deep breath. Perhaps Mary Ann was right about this grandma. I needed to think more about the sunny side and how it could help me. After a while, I eased up a bit, so now I felt ready in my heart to spend some time with this grandma, who to me was an unknown person and a complete stranger. I asked, "When can she pick me up?"

"I need to call her and she can be here in a few days." Mary Ann replied.

"Can I take my cars?"

"Yes, Henry, you can take all your cars and the new clothes, too."

Saturday, November 20, 1976 (Ten days later)

Jessa Odin returned to the children's home.

"Hello Ms. Odin, I am so happy to see you. Did you bring the court documents with you? I need to make sure we haven't missed anything."

"Right here."

"It's a good thing we could get into court last week to get your temporary legal guardianship, otherwise we would have had to wait a few more weeks."

"Where is Henry?"

"He is in his room packing all his toys. He has accumulated quite a collection."

"His other stuff?"

"I packed up some new clothes in a bag. Someone came in the other day and donated two bags of children's clothing. The only item we weren't able to get for him were shoes. He's been wearing the same pair for a while."

"That's ok, I'll find him a pair."

"Ok then, let's go get Henry."

Mary Ann and Jessa entered the room to find me sitting on the bed.

Wearing my favorite red shirt, holding on to a bag of stuff. I had no choice but to accept this new future of unknowns. My heart and my head were in a chaotic state. I felt tired of being shuffled back and forth to this place. As nice as Mary Ann was, I cared very little for this place, and even less for the kids here. My heart and I needed a normal life like my friend Tony. A home where we could play with the best toys and eat the best foods, and yet what I wanted the most was for my mom to love me. Take a deep breath. Hands fidget. Count the tile squares on the floor.

Mary Ann tried to keep her composure when she said, "Henry, your grandma is here to pick you up."

I looked straight at Jessa, or rather grandma and asked her, "Can you buy me ice cream?"

Grandma's eyes teared up. "Yes, Henry, I will get you any ice cream you want."

Grandma took me by the hand. Upon reaching the front door, I ran back to Mary Ann. Gave her one last hug and said to her, "Can you tell my mom I went to my grandma's house?"

She choked on her tears. "Yes Henry, I will." She tucked in my loose strands one last time. Hugged me and whispered, "You are going to be fine. Your grandma is going to take good care of you."

She regained her composure. Stood by the door, waved goodbye. I too waved back and wondered if I would ever see Mary Ann again. She had become an angel to so many kids, including me. Was always there to pick us up. Help us maneuver through the storms in our lives.

The moment I settled into grandma's car, I asked, "Grandma, can you take me to my house?"

"That's where we are going. I want to go get you some more things." Grandma said.

Happiness stepped in right next to me.

I couldn't contain myself in the back seat. "Grandma, if my mom is there, I can stay with her. I don't have to go with you anymore."

She smiled as she pretended not to hear the last of my words.

A short time later, grandma drove up to an old apartment building. "Ok Henry, let's go to the office to see if someone can open the apartment for us."

We walked in to find a young woman sitting at a desk doing something with her nails. It looked somewhat painful. I quickly shoved my hands in my pockets.

Grandma spoke first, "Hi, I'm Liset Odin's mother, I need to get some things out of apartment P22."

The young woman blew the dust off the desk. "Liset Odin? Isn't that the lady who disappeared about a month ago?"

"Yes, my daughter."

"Did they ever find her?"

"No, not yet."

"That's so sad and for the little boy, too."

"The little boy is my grandson. Can we get into the apartment?"

"What apartment was it again?"

"P22."

"Let me check the file."

She pulled out a folder stuffed with papers.

Looking like this might take longer than expected, Grandma and I took to sitting on some weathered looking chairs. I played with the thread on the cushion. Several minutes later, the girl asked, "What apartment did you say?"

Grandma cleared her throat, trying to stay calm. "P22." She called out.

"Yeah, so it looks like apartment P22 is now under a new tenant's name."

Grandma stood up. "What? No, that can't be right."

"It says here Liset Odin was behind on the rent by three months. Management had to vacate the apartment."

"So Liset never returned?"

"No ma'am, we kept leaving notices for her. She never responded or came by."

Grandma was growing concerned. "What did you do with the furniture and clothes?"

"The maintenance people take care of that. They have garage sales. If there is anything left after that, then they donate it to charity."

I couldn't understand anything they were saying. I pulled on grandma's arm, "Can we go see if mom is there?" I asked her.

Grandma led me back to the car in silence.

"Grandma, what's wrong?"

"Henry, the apartment is now clean and someone else's."

"No grandma. Mom is there. We have to go see."

She responded in a choked up voice, "No Henry, she's not there. Your mom never came back."

I sat back in the seat, feeling as if someone had just punched all the air out of me. Couldn't breathe. Couldn't breathe. Take a deep breath. Take a deep breath. Hands fidget. My home and everything in it were gone, just like my mom. I cried out, "Mom! I want my mom!"

Grandma started the car. Turned the radio on. Got back on the road. I found myself ignored and silenced by the blaring music. I stopped crying. Spent the rest of the drive with my head pressed to the window. The outside world looked like a blur. Car was moving too fast. My eyes couldn't focus on anything. People on streets looked confused and lost. Maybe my mom was out there too. I wanted to jump out of the car and go look for her. A short time later, I abandoned the thought when grandma's car came to a complete stop.

The house with the chain-link fence looked nothing like my apartment building with the smelly dumpster. Underneath the crooked branches, the house looked like it had way more windows than my tiny apartment. Grass, weeds were much more attractive than a dirty slab of cement. Pressed my face to the window, eyeing the walkway. Partially covered in vegetation, it had the look of something gone wrong. How could Mary Ann tell me grandma's house was pretty? This house looked scary. Just when my anxiety was about to kick in, I noticed the two rocking chairs sitting on the front porch. One was much smaller. Painted in my favorite color of red. Maybe this could be a good sign. I pulled away from the window.

"Grandma, is this your house?"

"Yes, Henry."

"How do we get in?"

Grandma opened the car door. "I have a key to the gate. Don't forget your toy. Around here we can't leave anything in our cars."

"Why grandma?"

"Things disappear. We never see them again."

"Are they going to take me too?"

"No Henry, not you. Just the stuff you leave behind. Let's go inside."

Once inside, grandma's scratchy voice said, "We need some sunshine in here. Let's open the curtains."

My worried eyes scanned the room. Take a deep breath. Take a deep breath. Hands fidget. Novelty knick-knacks adorned the walls. Lace covered the small coffee tables. Some sort of clear plastic material covered the sofa and the two chairs. An old looking wooden box occupied the area by the corner windows. Perhaps that was the television.

I pinched my nose and turned away.

"What's wrong Henry?"

"It smells in here."

Grandma laughed. "It's an old house with old things. Come on, let's go see your room."

A dark, paneled hallway led us to the back of the house. Grandma unlocked a door. Pushed it open. Not much better in here, either. I pinched my nose again. I stood there, assessing the room that was going to be mine for the time being. Maybe it would not be permanent. Take a deep breath. Hands fidget. Dark panels covered the walls, similar to the hallway. Neatly folded over the bed was an old patched up quilt. A stuffed bear leaned on a pillow. The dresser was a bit worn but looked to have enough space for all my new stuff. To my dismay, the only window in the room appeared to have crunched up tin foil taped to it. There would be no bird watching from this window, for sure. How could I get excited about having my room and sleeping in an actual bed, if the room had dark walls and a covered window? What was Mary Ann thinking when she said grandma's house was pretty? Obviously, she hadn't seen the inside. And especially not the room grandma had just gifted me.

"What do you think, Henry?"

Take a deep breath. Hands fidget.

"What's wrong?"

"I don't like it. It's old. There's nothing new."

She crossed her arms and laughed. "My house may be old and smelly like me, but I wouldn't trade it for anything else. Many years ago, when I didn't have a place to live, God found this house for me and now you get to live in it too."

Clock on the wall chimed. "Oh no, I'm missing my show. Henry, put your things in the dresser. In this house, we don't leave things scattered around. I'm old and I can trip and fall."

I became fearful at hearing her tone. "Grandma, are you going to hurt me?"

"No Henry, I could never hurt you. You're my only grandson. Did your mom hurt you?"

My eyes teared up.

She wrapped her arms around me and said. "We will not worry anymore, because God is holding on to you and I from now on."

Wiped my teary eyes with the back of my hand as she continued talking, "In this house, no one is going to hurt you. God is with us, so stop crying already. I'm missing my show on television. You can stay here and play with your cars or come sit with me."

I emptied my bag on the bed. Gathered as many cars as my small arms could hold.

Followed grandma back into the living room where she had taken to her rocking chair.

She motioned, "Henry, come sit on the sofa."

No sooner had I dumped all the cars on the sofa than turned my attention to the knickknacks on the wall. The metal buggy would make a perfect addition to my new collection of cars.

Noting what I was about to do, grandma darted out of her chair, "Oh no, those are not for play. Give it here."

I wasn't about to let go of it that easily. I wanted the opportunity to play with it. Assess the cool wheels. Could it race as fast as my new red car? The opportunity, however, was not in my favor. Grandma stood towering over me. She wrinkled her face at me. Extended her hand, "Henry, let me have it. I will put it back." She said.

I lost the battle. Expressed a sad face. Plumped myself on the sofa. "Grandma, why does your sofa make this noise?"

"Henry, I can't hear the television. Sit on the floor. You can play better on the floor with your cars."

I didn't mind the floor so much since my cars were all new with great spinning wheels. From the corner of my eye, I could tell grandma sure had an interest on the television. Volume was louder than Tony's television. Inside this television, people were talking in a language I didn't understand. Grandma sure seemed to enjoy it, though, because now and then she would burst out laughing.

After the show ended, grandma turned her attention back to me. "Are you hungry?"

I nodded. Of course I was hungry. I would never pass up food, no matter what it was.

I followed grandma into the kitchen. My hunger pains kicked in the moment I saw the assortment of cookies on the table. I took a seat. Scooted the cookie platter over to my side so I could study the variety. Round cookies with frosting looked pretty good. Square cookies with sprinkles are always a favorite at Christmas time. Which one to eat first? I picked the one with the sweet strawberry scent. Held it in my hand and then crushed it in my mouth.

"Henry, no cookies until you eat dinner."

Wiped my mouth clean of all crumbs.

Minutes later, a delicious aroma filled the kitchen. The tiny radio on the window seal began blaring music in the background. I couldn't ever remember my mom taking to the kitchen like grandma. In fact, mom spent no time in the kitchen, other than piling trash or cooling her favorite beverage.

Grandma was even a fast cook. In no time, she had prepared a meal on pretty floral plates. "Ok Henry, let's eat." She said.

The mouthwatering plate she put in front of me had the perfect meal for my tummy. It consisted of homemade tortillas, along with delicious spicy rice and well-seasoned beans and all nicely separated on the plate. I savored each tasty bite. Even ate whatever crumbs were left on the plate. At one point, I noticed grandma poured herself a different drink, so I asked, "Grandma, what are you drinking?"

"Red soda."

"Can I have some?"

"Are you finished eating all your food?"

I nodded.

"Then you can have some soda with your cookies."

Being in this house, with grandma, having actual food in the kitchen was a clear sign love was living here. Just like Tony's house. My home didn't have any of that. My mom didn't care to have love in our home. Maybe grandma could teach mom how to invite love in.

Jessa was the first one to finish eating. She looked over at Henry as he savored each bite of his cookie. Never had she seen a child so starved for food. Wondered what his life might be like at home, but then stopped herself short of thinking any further about the situation. She didn't want to get involved in her daughter's life or Henry's life, so she redirected her thoughts back to the present.

"Grandma, what is abortion?" Henry asked.

Grandma drew her eyebrows in, "What? What did you say?"

"Mom said she wanted an abortion, but the hospital told her no."

Grandma's demeanor changed at that moment. She quickly removed herself from the table and went to clean her plate in the sink.

I followed her. "Grandma, are you crying?"

"Sometimes people's words are confusing. I think your mom may not have been feeling well when she talked to you. Go finish your food."

I didn't understand why she couldn't tell me what the word abortion meant. It's just a word. Right? And what did it have to do with me, anyway? After a bit, I dismissed it. Cleaned my plate of any leftover crumbs. Hugged grandma and told her, "Grandma, you make good food."

She held on to me. Feeling her calm and caring spirit made all the difference in my small world.

From that moment on, Jessa Odin knew she would have to keep Henry with her even if it meant having to fight her daughter in court.

After washing dishes and sweeping floors, grandma took to the comfort of her rocker again.

"Grandma, what are you doing?"

"I'm going to read my bible."

"What's that?"

She removed her glasses. "The bible tells the story of God."

"Who is that, grandma?"

"He created earth and everything on it, including heaven."

"Where is heaven, grandma?"

"In the sky."

"Where the clouds are?"

"Yes, heaven is in the clouds."

"I want to go see it. Can you take me?"

Grandma laughed, "It's not that easy to get there."

"Why?"

"Because God wants us to have clean hearts first."

I looked at grandma, somewhat confused, "How do I clean my heart?" I asked.

"Well, you need to tell people you're sorry if you hurt them."

"But I didn't hurt nobody."

Grandma put her arms around me. "What I mean is you should always try to be nice to people, try to be a good helper if you can."

I scratched my head, "That's too much words. They make my head hurt."

Grandma laughed, "One day you will understand. Play with your cars, Henry."

"Grandma, when is mom coming back?"

"I don't know, but I think we should start lighting a candle for her every night when we pray."

"Can we go look for her?"

"Henry, the police are looking for her. They will bring her back when they find her."

At that moment, grandma yawned, said she was feeling tired and felt like going to her room to lie down to take a nap.

I continued playing with my cars, but after a while I grew bored and went looking for grandma.

Knocked on her door. "Grandma, what are you doing?" No answer. I tried again. "Grandma?" She didn't respond. Decided to open the door myself. Saw her on her knees, I rushed in. "Grandma, did you fall?"

"No Henry, I lit the small candle and now I'm praying."

"What's praying?"

"It means I'm talking to God. I'm asking him to take care of my friends and to keep looking for your mom."

"Grandma, what does he look like?"

"Who?"

"God."

"Well, it's not about what he looks like, but what he is. He is the sunshine in the sky and the pretty flower outside my window. He is the smile I see in your eyes when you play with your cars."

That made little sense to this eight-year-old. I threw my arms up in the air. "I don't know what you're saying."

She winked at me. "One day you will, but for now, let's pray. Here, take your hands and clap them together. Tell God about your mom."

"What do I tell him?"

"Tell him how you miss her. Tell him you want her back."

"Ok."

Minutes later, grandma pulled herself up and sat on her bed. She sighed, then said, "Henry, we need to get your clothes ready for tomorrow."

"What's tomorrow grandma?"

"We go to church."

"What's that?"

"You'll see when we get there."

CHAPTER ELEVEN

Sunday, November 21, 1976

"Henry, you need to wake up. We are losing time. I don't like being late to church, then someone else will get my parking spot."

I pulled the covers over my head. Rolled over to the opposite side of the bed.

"Henry."

I peeked my head out from under the covers. "Where are we going?" I asked.

"Church and then to go get some things I need."

"Church?"

"You'll see when we get there."

Once inside the car, the excitement set in and I began wiggling around the back seat. I had never been to some place called church. I asked all the right questions. "Do they have toys there? Grandma, is it a scary place? Is there going to be lots of people? Will there be someone I can play with? I'm hungry."

Grandma smiled as she pulled into her favorite parking spot in front of the church.

"Henry, stop asking so many questions. You will see when we walk inside."

The white building didn't appear to be a house. In fact, it looked like a triangle. Looking out the window, I caught sight of something and asked, "What's that?"

Grandma turned around to see what I was referring to. "Oh, you mean the cross?"

"Why is it so big? What if it falls and hits us?"

"Henry, the cross will not fall. It's there to let people know this is a special house."

"Special? How grandma?"

"It means anyone who sees it from far away can come here to learn about how God can help them find love and peace in their lives."

"Grandma, is God in there? Can he help us find mom?"

"Your mom never talked to you about God?"

"Who?"

Grandma fixed her watch on her wrist, "It's time to go inside and find our seats."

The front doors were tall. They displayed carvings of a man carrying a cross with people around him. I couldn't help but touch. As I'm sure everyone else does when they walk through these doors. I felt a cool breeze brush past my cheeks the moment I stepped inside. My heart began racing. Take a deep breath. Take a deep breath. What was this place? My eyes scanned the room for details. There were colorful stained glass windows. The morning sun filtered in, creating rainbows throughout the room. Soft green carpet paved the way to the big room with rows and rows of long wooden benches. In one corner sat a grand piano. On the opposite side a couple gathered around a votive candle rack to pray. Front center, a large cross was on display underneath a bright light.

"Grandma, why does this house look like this? I don't see a television. Where are the toys?"

"Come Henry, let's sit close to the front, so we can hear better."

"Grandma, who are these people?"

"Henry, stop asking questions."

Grandma and I took our seats in the second row from the front while everyone else sat behind us. We would have no problems hearing whoever was going to talk to us about whatever they talk about at a place like this.

Grandma urged me to put my hands together to pray. She said to me, "Start talking to God. Ask him to find your mom."

"Grandma, how come we can't see him?"

"Henry, you don't have to see God to believe he is here. You just feel him in your heart, just like when you play with your cars. You feel happy, don't you?"

I nodded.

"Ok then, that happy you feel in your heart is God. And now I need to pray. Here play with your car. Need to figure out what I'm going to say to God."

Did what grandma told me to do, picked up my car but kept thinking about my mom. Missing her. Wishing she was here with grandma and me.

Moments later, a man walked up to the piano. Made a brief announcement. Sat down to play music. People stood up and began singing, clapping only to have it cut short by a burley man who appeared through the side door. He held a book in his hand, speaking in a tone as if no one could hear him.

I tapped grandma on the shoulder. "Grandma, why is he mad?"

She said to me, "Henry, he makes his voice sound loud so people will listen to him."

"He is scaring me. Can we go home now?"

"In a little while, Henry."

I did not know what he was talking about the entire time we were present. Apparently, everyone else did because they would respond with the word amen quite frequently. Another word I knew nothing about.

After church came to a close, grandma turned to me with her kind smile and asked, "Did you like church?"

I made a face, "No."

"Why not?"

"There were no toys. I never saw God, think he was hiding."

Grandma winked back at me as she led me out the door.

We walked across the parking lot to a building marked with the lettering Family Hope Center.

At eight-years-old I was just full of questions, "Where are we going?"

"It's a surprise."

"What is it, grandma?"

"Well, as soon as the line gets short, we can go inside. I'll show you."

I couldn't contain my excitement. "Do they have toys here? Do they have food? I'm Hungry."

"Just wait Henry. It's almost our turn to go inside, and then I can get you some cookies."

An hour later, grandma and I stepped inside. They gave us coupons to use for food and clothing. Grandma picked up two boxes stuffed with some weird food, along with a watermelon and a box of some smelly soap. Maybe something good would come out of all this.

Grandma and I then made our way to a much smaller building. The moment we stepped inside, I encountered a weird smell. I pinched my nose. The smell didn't seem to bother grandma though; she just kept walking through the aisles and aisles of stuff. She hummed the same tune we had just heard in church. Along the way, she would stop to admire a few pieces of clothing. If she liked them, she would put them in the basket; otherwise, she would put them back on the rack. She kept humming the same tune over and over. This went on for quite a while. I was getting anxious. I had never been to a place like this before. There had to be more than just clothes. I wanted to see what else was around the corner.

"Grandma, do they have toys here?"

She winked at me for the second time and said, "Maybe. Let's go check out the shelves back in the corner."

My eyes lit up the moment I saw the shelves. Never had I seen so many toys spilling from stacked shelves. Feeling like I had stepped into toy heaven, I couldn't decide which one to look at first. Running to grandma then back to the toys, I started assessing them all with the hope I could find some cool ones. And then maybe by some miracle I could convince grandma to buy me at least one if not more. I picked up a dump truck. "Grandma, can I play with this one? It has good wheels. Grandma, can I have this one?"

"I don't know if I can buy toys with these coupons."

"Please grandma, I want one."

"Hold on Henry. Don't be taking everything off the shelves. I have to ask."

Well worth the time spent at this place because grandma and I piled clothing items and several toys into the small basket. Just when I thought we were done and ready to leave, grandma looked at her shopping list one last time and said, "I have one more item to pick up. Henry, let's walk over to the shoe area."

What an eventful day, church, toys and now shoes. The lengthy time spent on a church bench listening to a man with a loud voice didn't seem so bad now. I could get used to this. Particularly if it meant I could get new toys and shoes.

"Grandma, can you buy me some shoes? Look, grandma mine are broken."

"That's why we're here."

I tried on several pairs of shoes. None were destined to be mine. They were the wrong size, or I didn't like the color. Others had those hard to tie shoelaces. I was about to give up hope but then grandma took to a pile of shoes stacked on the side of the room. Underneath, she found a pair of clean and gently used sport shoes. My face lit up. The shoes had red stripes and way too long orange shoelaces. I tried them on anyway.

"Look grandma, I can run fast."

She laughed, "Yes, you can."

"I want them, grandma. Please, can I have them?"

"Yes, Henry, you can have them. They will be good for school."

The shoes were the perfect fit. No longer was I going to be walking around in broken shoes with holes. I could now race Tony and all the kids at school and no one was going to laugh at me again.

I held on to grandma's hand as we headed back to the car. At one point, I turned to her and said, "Grandma, I have new toys now. I never had new toys before."

Grandma's eyes teared up as she ushered me into the car.

Chapter Twelve

Monday, November 22, 1976

Morning arrived with fear in the air. Grandma led me by the hand into a school building I had never seen before. The hallways were long and skinny. Faces of other kids were unfamiliar. Feeling lost and confused, I didn't like this at all. Take a deep breath. Hands fidget. I wanted to go back to my school to see my friend Tony. I miss my teacher, Ms. Ramos. She was always nice to me. I felt safer there than I did anywhere else. This place didn't have the same feeling. I pulled grandma's hand back.

She pulled me forward. "Let's hurry Henry. The tardy bell rang and now you're late."

"I want to go to my school."

"Henry, the other school is in the city. It's too far."

"I want to see my friend Tony."

"You'll make some new friends here."

"Can I just stay home with you? I don't like this school."

"You'll get used to this school. You'll make

new friends. Come on. I think this is the classroom we're looking for."

"Are you coming back for me?"

"I'm going to be right outside the school doors when the bell rings this afternoon."

My eyes welled up with tears. "You promise?"

"Yes Henry, I promise."

A soft voice cut into our conversation, "Hello, I'm Ms. Carol."

I stepped back and hid behind grandma.

Grandma nudged me forward. "Look Henry, this is your teacher, Ms. Carol."

Teacher moved closer, "Hello Henry. Welcome to your new classroom."

I looked back to make sure grandma was still there. Take a deep breath. Take a deep breath. Hands fidget. Count squares on floor.

"What's wrong Henry?"

Grandma piped in, "Henry gets anxious when he's unfamiliar with something or someone. He just needs a moment to take a deep breath and focus. He'll be fine."

Teacher reached for my hand, "Come along Henry, your new friends are excited to meet you."

I moved back, "No."

Teacher continued, "We have an exciting day planned. This morning we will get a visit from our science friends, who are bringing turtles and a very cool spider. Right now we are unpacking, getting ready for morning announcements, and then we are going to music class."

Grandma pulled me by the hand towards the classroom door again. "Come on Henry, let's go inside."

I clung to grandma as she ushered me into the classroom.

New classmates rushed over to greet me. Giving grandma an opportunity to stand back.

It wasn't but five minutes when I noticed grandma had disappeared. Be brave. Be brave. Being brave can help me. It was of no help. I broke out crying anyway.

Teacher came around to sit next to me, "Why are you crying, Henry?"

"My grandma is not coming back."

"Of course she is. Every day when school is over, your grandma will be outside waiting for you, just as she promised."

"I want to go home."

"I'm sorry Henry. You come to school, so you can learn new things and make new friends. And right now we are getting ready to go to music class." She turned her attention back to the other students. "Ok class, announcements are over. It's time to line up."

I had a better idea. I bolted out of my chair. Ran out of the classroom into the hallway. Ran as fast as I could, hoping to find a door leading to the outside. I got rather lucky when I turned a corner and soon enough found a door. I pushed as hard as I could until it opened. At last I was free. I ran around the building only to see two adults coming in my direction. Tried to run faster. It was of no use. The adults had faster shoes.

They caught up to me, "Henry, where are you going?"

"I don't like it here. I want to go home."

"Henry, you must stay in school."

"I want my grandma."

"Your grandma will pick you up after school."

By midday, the vice principal had taken charge of my dire situation. "Henry, we can't have you running out the door every few minutes. Everyone is tiring of chasing you around the building. Because of this, you now have to sit in my office."

"I want my grandma."

"I just called her. She's on her way."

Grandma walked into the vice principal's office to find me sitting at a small desk. The moment I saw her, I bolted out of the chair and ran to her. I clung to her like cement glue. No one was going to pull me away from my grandma. Not now. Not Never. She wrapped her arms around me. "Henry, I'm so sorry you are having a hard time. You can't just go running out of school doors. It would make me very sad if something were to happen to you. I told you I would not leave you, like your mom did. Every day I will be here to pick you up." Her eyes teared up as she said to me, "I love you." It was the first time in my entire young life someone had ever addressed those three brief words to me. My mom never used them in front of me. Yet I had heard them plenty of times when parents would drop off their kids at school. Even at Tony's house. His mom and dad were always saying those words. I hugged my grandma, hoping I would remember this moment forever.

In just a matter of days, grandma had taken to caring and loving me as her own. Me, a scrawny kid with a head full of messed up hair. I no longer was just some kid pushed to the side like a piece of trash. I mattered to someone. That someone was my grandma. If only other kids could be so lucky.

CHAPTER THIRTEEN

Thursday, November 25, 1976
(Three days later)

"Henry, stop staring out the window and come finish your homework."

"I can't do it."

"What is it you can't do?"

"Too much numbers. They hurt my brain."

"It doesn't matter if you can't do it the way the teacher wants you to. Grab the pencil and scribble something on the paper. Teacher can't give you a poor mark for trying."

I shifted my attention from my mom to my homework, then back to my grandma. I pulled away from the window. "Grandma, how come I never met you before?"

"Your mom and me never could get along. I spent a good part of my life out on the street with my friends and never paid much attention to Liset when she was growing up."

Grandma took a tissue out of her pocket and continued, "Your mom, she didn't like me telling her what to do. One day, she packed up her clothes. Said she was going to live with her friends. That was the last I heard of her."

"Grandma, how come you didn't go look for her?"

Grandma wiped her eyes. "Back then, I didn't care and was busy having a good time with my friends. My friends were more important than my little girl. If I could go back in time, I would have chosen my little girl. Things might be different between us right now. And maybe, just maybe, we might all be together right now."

Grandma wiped her face again. "It's enough talking about me. Let's go back to your math homework. If you scribble something on that paper and sit quietly while I watch my show, later I will buy you a cone from the ice cream truck."

I didn't hesitate in saying "Okay grandma." Ice cream is a rare thing in my world. I get ice cream at Tony's house or in school when the teacher treats us for doing all our work. Today, when grandma offered to buy me a cone, I made every attempt to complete whatever I could on the math homework. Scribbled some numbers on the paper just like grandma told me to do. Even sat quietly and didn't move an inch on the plastic covered sofa.

Thirty minutes later, grandma and I stood on the sidewalk waiting for the ice cream truck to arrive at our stop. In the time we waited, I noticed the house across the street had people walking around on the side lawn. I could see kids sitting at a long table covered in a bright red tablecloth. At one end of the table sat a boy with a giant hat waiting while a lady placed a candle lit cake in front of him.

I pulled on grandma's shirt, "Grandma, there's a party over there."

"I see. Looks like a birthday party for a boy. Ok Henry, the ice cream truck is here. Do you want a chocolate or vanilla cone?"

Shrugged my shoulders, an indication I'd lost interest in the ice cream.

"What's wrong Henry?"

"I don't want ice cream anymore."

"Yes you do Henry, here I'll get you the vanilla."

Instead, I ran back into the house and straight to my darkroom. I threw myself on the bed. Turned to face the wall, hoping to hide my teary eyes before grandma could see them.

Grandma followed right behind as fast as she could, holding onto the ice cream cone. "Henry, what's wrong?"

How to begin? Should I even ask? Yet I felt like I had to know so I spilled my words, "Grandma, do I have a birthday?"

"Everyone has a birthday. Did your mom not give you a birthday party?"

"No."

"I'm so sorry, Henry. I will see what I can do so you can have a birthday party."

My eyes lit up, "Really grandma? With balloons and a cake?"

"Yes. We can invite your friends. Right now, though, you better grab the ice cream cone and eat it before it melts."

At that moment, I felt as if happy had stepped right back into my life. I wanted to do things. I wanted to go places. "Grandma, can you take me to the movies? I want to go. I never have seen a movie. My friend Tony told me the movie is on a giant wall. He says it's bigger than a house. Can you take me? I want to go."

"I don't know Henry. Right now, I don't have a lot of money. I need to save my money for food, to pay my bills and now for your special day."

Well, so much for happy, just as soon as happy had arrived, it had left. I threw myself on the sofa. "Grandma, you're boring."

Grandma removed her eyeglasses, "Yes, I know I'm boring. Back when I was young, I never thought I was going to get old. Never did I think I was going to need money like I do now. Back in those days when I was young, I only thought of having a good time with my friends enjoying the moment and nothing else."

"But grandma..."

"No more talking Henry, I don't want to

bring anymore sadness into our lives with details of my past mistakes."

Two hours later.

"Henry, it's time for bed. You have school
tomorrow."

"Grandma, we forgot the candle for mom."

"Oh yes, I'm sorry."

I wanted to feel like I was contributing to
this prayer thing, so I asked, "Can we put it in
my room tonight?"

"Yes, we can light the candle and pray in
your room."

"Can I play with my red car, too?"

"Well, not while we pray. God doesn't like
distractions. He wants all of your attention. You
can play with it after prayer. After that, it's time
to go to sleep."

I made a face, "Ok grandma."

We lit the candle, prayed, and then grandma
tucked me in. She whispered the magic words,
"I love you." Closed the door behind her.

I closed my eyes and smiled all the way to the
night sky.

Instead of going straight to bed, Jessa Odin
spent some quiet time in her rocking chair. She
opened her bible and made a plea to God, "Help me
please, so I can raise my grandson. I'm all he has."

CHAPTER FOURTEEN

Thursday, May 25, 1977 (Six months later)

The afternoon school bell rang and within a matter of minutes, the teacher shuffled my classmates and me through the hallways and out the glass doors. Grandma was waiting in her car by the curve as she had been doing for the past six months. I jumped into the back seat next to a bouquet of balloons.

"Grandma, what are the balloons for?"

She smiled. "We have a party to go to."

I could hardly contain my excitement. "Where is it, grandma?"

"You'll see when we get home."

The drive home was only a few blocks away, yet today it was taking an eternity to get there. Grandma kept encountering extra stop signs along the way.

"Grandma, can you go faster?"

She laughed, "Henry, my car is old like me. We aren't as shiny and fast as we used to be."

The moment we arrived home, I bolted out of the car. "Grandma, what are all the cars for?"

She winked at me. "It's for the party."

"What party, grandma?"

"The party at our house."

I ran inside the house only to find the rooms were dark and quiet. As I neared the kitchen, I could hear conversations coming from the backyard. Opened the back door just as grandma was coming up the steps with the bouquet of balloons shouting, "SURPRISE!"

"For me, grandma?"

She hugged me, "Happy Birthday Henry."

"It's my birthday, grandma?"

"Yes Henry, today you are nine-years-old. Go have some fun."

I set out to assess the backyard. Adults scattered around the yard were in deep conversation while kids played tag. It all seemed inviting, yet it was the table dressed in blue that garnered most of my attention. Painted with a delicious blend of foods. My favorite food - spicy sausages smothered in red sauce on a tray for all to see. Triangle shaped sandwiches with chips decorated the other side of the table. Grandma's delicious spicy rice was sitting pretty in a blue bowl. I continued moving along, taking in the smell of fresh baked beans. And who could forget the baked bread in baskets? The butter looked perfect. I swiped a quick lick. Trays filled with a variety of sweet treats finished the pretty table. I picked up a homemade cookie. Took in the sweet scent of cinnamon, crushing it in my mouth. The table on the opposite side, displaying seasonal fruit, looked rather inviting, too. I grabbed a handful of juicy watermelon balls. Clearly, this was the way to a happy heart. I turned the corner of the house to see grandma's old tree draped in red streamers. There it was; a giant Piñata in the shape of a red car hanging from a branch. Couldn't resist. I strolled over. Punched it as hard as I could. Hoping to see candy or toys of some sort fall out, but nothing came out.

Jessa held on to her tears as she watched her only grandson from a distance, who was very much having the best time of his life. She hoped to remember this moment forever.

I came running back as soon as I saw grandma, "Where's the cake?" I asked.

Grandma cleared her throat. "If you go find your chair, I'll bring the cake out."

Grandma placed the decorated cake in front of me. I beamed with excitement as I said, "Grandma, it looks just like my red car!"

"Yes, it does Henry."

Kids gathered around to sing Happy Birthday, bringing my heart the biggest happy ever.

To keep the momentum going, grandma

piled all the gifts next to me. "Grandma, are they all for me?" I asked.

Teary-eyed again, she responded, "Yes, they are all for you."

Cake, ice cream and a load of gifts were all pleasing to my heart, yet I was eager to take on the last part of the party. Sometime later, grandma lined us kids by the old tree ready to take on the piñata with a stick. The kids and I had hoped to empty the piñata of all the sweet treats, but failed just after a few brief attempts. Grandma had to step in and help. She saved the moment by smashing the piñata for us. I stuffed as many treats as my pockets could hold, forcing grandma to call me out, "Henry, don't be greedy. Save some for your friends."

Hours later, after everyone had left the party; Jessa and Henry sat on the back patio steps exhausted but very content. Henry played with his stack of new cars, and Jessa's thoughts drifted back into the past, forcing her to recall the biggest mistake of her life. Not having been around to give her daughter the love she needed when she was young. And now her daughter had done the same thing. At that moment Jessa Odin's heart reached out to God, asking for forgiveness.

CHAPTER FIFTEEN

Friday, February 6, 1981 (Five years later)

"Henry, why is it when I call you, you don't respond? You don't seem to want to listen for nothing. You don't hear me because your long hair is in your face all the time. To hear me better, I need to take you to get a haircut."

I made my usual face and rolled my eyes. I needed to stretch a bit more on the sofa. Today I wasn't in the mood to listen to grandma's chatter and especially not if she was just spilling words for the sake of talking.

"Henry, go look at the calendar in the kitchen. What day it is?"

"Grandma, it's so much work to get up. You do it."

"Henry, just do it."

"It's February six, grandma."

Grandma stared into her coffee cup and then gave me that look of despair and said, "It is the start of another year. The time is passing. You're now in middle school. Your birthday is around the corner too. Your mom has lost the best years of your childhood." She wiped her teary eyes, "Every day, I ask God to bring us word of your mom so we can know something. This waiting around is hard. It's hard on me. I know it's hard on you, too."

Grandma's rambling was making me feel restless. It was time to take a break.

"Grandma, can I go see my friends?"

"Friends? Where?"

"Around the corner."

"And what are you going to do with those friends?"

"I don't know. Maybe go walk to the store or just hangout."

"Henry, I've seen those friends of yours. They don't look like good friends. They look like troublemakers."

"Come on grandma, let me go. It's just for a little while. I promise I won't be gone long."

"Henry, I'm not feeling well. Maybe you should stay here with me."

"Grandma, we go nowhere. There is never money to do anything. I'm tired of sitting here by the window. Staring, waiting for mom to come back. We live boring lives. Come on, let me go."

Grandma was giving me the look again. The look meant she was preparing to give me one of her long-winded speeches. I made a face.

She pointed her finger at me, "Just because

there is no money in this house like your friends have in their houses doesn't make us boring people. We can do a lot of things without money."

I rolled my eyes, "Like what, grandma?"

"Go cut the grass. You can help me with that. You never want to help me cut the grass."

I curled my lips.

"You can clean your room too. I walk in there. I can't find your bed anymore."

"Grandma, those are chores. I want to do something fun."

She removed her eyeglasses; "It's not so good to be thinking about having fun all the time. You need to be thinking more about God."

"Yes, yes, I know. You preach to me a million times a day. I'm only a kid. Why do I have to be thinking about God right now?"

"Because one day you're going to be an adult and life may get hard. Who is going to be there to help you?"

"You are grandma."

"We can't live forever, Henry. God decides when it's time. And for me, it could be any time."

All this talking was making me feel anxious. I looked out the window and turned back to grandma, "My friend is out there waiting. Can I go?"

She had to look out the window too. My word was never enough.

She said, "Okay, but only for one hour. The

time on the clock is five. You come back in one hour. I'm going to go lay down in my room. Wake me up when you get back. I will make dinner."

Before she could finish talking, I dashed out the door as fast as I could. I had freedom for one hour, which meant I could do anything I wanted to. Well, sort of. Ten dollars would not get me a ride to the beach or somewhere cool. I settled for hanging out with my friends. Sitting on the curve. Talking about stupid stuff like girls. Complaining about doing chores. Wandering what our adult lives would look like in ten years. Would we still be friends?

The hour came and went and Henry didn't return home as promised.

Two hours later.

Somewhere in the midst of laughing and eating an ice cream cone, I lost track of time. The house was dark and quiet when I returned home. I imagined grandma was still in her room sleeping. I knocked on her door. No response. I knocked again. Nothing. This time, I pushed the door open. Grandma was lying on the floor. "Grandma, what's wrong?" She was unresponsive. My efforts to help her proved useless. I was a kid who knew nothing. I grabbed the phone and called for help instead. Take a deep breath. Take a deep breath. Hands fidget.

Paramedics arrived with their equipment in hand. Watching them attend to grandma, my heart started racing. At one point one of them asked me, "Do you know if she is taking any medications? Your grandma's pulse is very weak."

I didn't know how to respond because I was a kid and besides; I had never given a thought to grandma getting sick. She always seemed fine to me. She laughed and talked like any normal person.

I stumbled on my words, "I, I don't know."

The paramedic continued, "Your grandma appears to be very ill. We will have to transport her to a hospital."

Take a deep breath. Take a deep breath. Hands fidget. "Can I go too?" I asked.

Paramedic looked at me, "Are you okay?"

"When I get anxious about stuff, I have to take a deep breath a few times so I can get myself to calm down."

"Sounds like you have anxiety."

"Yes, a little sometimes." I replied.

"Sure, we can take you so you can be with your grandma."

I didn't want to get into any details about my childhood or my mother, so I went along with their suggestions and nodded.

CHAPTER SIXTEEN

The paramedics rolled the stretcher into the emergency room with me in tow. Not knowing what to expect, I settled for a seat in a quiet corner away from all the commotion until someone could come get me. Feeling anxious, I took to counting the square tiles on the floor. When that didn't calm me down, I turned to counting flowers around the waiting room. I found them in vases. I found them on artwork placed on the walls. Vibrant floral patterns dressed the seating throughout the room. Perhaps it too could keep me engaged until someone could tell me about grandma's condition. After a while, it did me no good. My mind began rambling inside my head. Would grandma be ok? How long would she have to stay in the hospital? How would we get home? Closed my eyes, trying to shut everyone and everything out so I could find some peace. I even prayed just as grandma had taught me to do. I wanted everything to be okay for grandma and me.

Not long after, a man dressed in a white lab coat appeared through the steel doors. He looked at his clipboard, glanced out into the waiting room and called for the Jessa Odin family.

Take a deep breath. Take a deep breath. I stood up.

"Are you related to Jessa Odin?"

"She's my grandma."

"Follow me, please."

"Is my grandma ok?"

"Well, no, she's very sick."

"What's wrong with her?" I asked.

"Your grandma has a condition called arrhythmia."

I scratched my head. "What's that?"

"It means her heart is not well. She may need surgery and a change of medication."

"Is she going to die?"

"Not right now. She's lucky to be alive. You saved your grandma's life. Had you waited any longer to call for help, she might not have made it."

"Can I see her?"

"Only for a few minutes. We are still securing her vitals."

Take a deep breath. Take a deep breath. Upon seeing my grandma lying on the sterile bed, my anxiety set in, causing me to clench my teeth. I felt like someone had just punched all the living air out of me. I swallowed what little saliva I had in my mouth over and over. Take a deep breath. Take a deep breath. I scanned her face, her hands, and her body for potential signs of life. Nothing. She was stiff. I choked back my cries. "Grandma, I'm afraid. Please don't die. I love you, grandma."

Overwhelmed with emotion, I ran out of the room, out of the hospital, and into the chilly night, couldn't see anything ahead of me, yet I could feel the cold air moving around me to the point of suffocation. Couldn't breathe. Couldn't breathe. I held on to a pole. Closed my eyes. Prayed to God just as grandma had taught me to do.

Moments later, the sounds of sirens interrupted my thoughts. The paramedics rushed to unload the stretchers from two ambulances. My eyes caught sight of a boy not much older than me. I could hear the paramedic shouting, "We've lost him! His pulse is gone!"

Lady on the other stretcher looked to be bleeding. Would she survive? I turned to God and prayed some more.

Sometime later that evening.

Henry arrived home feeling spent. He took to his grandma's rocking chair until he regained his composure. Afterwards, he headed straight to her bedroom because it was the only room in the house where he could feel her presence and take in her lingering sweet scent. He wrapped himself in her red scarf. Curled up in her bed. Fixed his eyes on the ceiling tiles, looking for some kind of distraction from the heaviness in his heart, but it was useless. The disoriented maze of broken pieces of tiles gave rise to his emotions once again. Cries of his broken heart echoed throughout the house.

CHAPTER SEVENTEEN

Friday, February 20, 1981 (Two weeks later)

Two weeks later, not much had changed other than grandma was still very much ill and in the hospital. I was finding it difficult to live alone in the house. I was on the verge of running out of food. How would I manage if I understood nothing about finances? I had no access to money. With no access to grandma's accounts, I did not know how or when to pay any of the utility bills. I dared not ask anyone at church for help, otherwise they would ask questions and someone might send me away.

Henry sat down to think some more, soon thereafter, a swift knock on the front door interrupted his thoughts. Fear set in as he tiptoed to a window to see a short man puffing away at a cigarette.

The short man knocked again. This time, his knock was louder. Hoping to get the neighborhood dogs' attention. Maybe it would wake somebody up so he could get the envelope delivered and be on his way to lunch.

Henry touched his chest, trying to calm his rapid heartbeat. Take a deep breath. Take a deep breath. What should he do? If he ignored the knocking, maybe the short man would go away.

The short man knocked again. This time even louder and now the neighborhood dogs were barking.

He had no choice but to open the door.

The short man spoke first. "I'm with the constable's office; I'm delivering some papers."

"Papers for what?" I asked.

"They are eviction papers."

I tucked my hair back. "Eviction papers?"

"We received notice Jessa Odin passed away two weeks ago. She arranged with the county to defer her taxes some years ago and upon her death, the county would take possession of her house if the taxes were still outstanding."

"My grandma didn't die. She's in the hospital."

The man ignored everything I was trying to tell him and just continued with his prepared message.

"It's something common among the elderly who are on fixed income and can't pay their taxes."

Take a deep breath. Take a deep breath. Hands fidget.

"Is your mom or dad home? I can speak to either one about it and see how they want to handle the situation."

I didn't know what to say, I stuttered, "They, well, they went to work."

The man looked at me, "So what's your parents' names?"

My heart was racing. I couldn't think fast enough.

"What's your name, son? Aren't you supposed to be in school right now?"

Feeling uneasy with all the questioning I simply replied with, "I'm not feeling well. I have to get back to bed." I closed the door and locked it.

The short man radioed in for help. Sometime later, a lady arrived to assist him.

She took her turn, knocking on the door.

Take a deep breath. Take a deep breath. I could feel my hands sweating. What should I do? I began pacing back and forth. Should I open the door again? What would they do to me? Or maybe I should just run out the back door. No one would catch me but then where would I go? My situation appeared hopeless.

The lady and the short man had no plans to leave. They continued knocking. At one point, the lady called out, "Hello, please open the door. We need to talk to you."

I caught my breath and picked up the phone. I had no choice but to call grandma's church. They could help me with this situation. They were always available to help everyone else with their problems. Why not me too? Sure enough, I called and the assistant minister agreed to help grandma and me, but for the time being I would have to go with these horrible people and wherever it was they wanted to take me. I feared the worst.

Henry took a deep breath. Pulled the door open. After the interrogation began, Henry felt like he had stepped into one of those courtroom shows his grandma enjoyed watching.

"What's your name, son?" The lady asked.

"Henry Odin." I replied.

"And your parents?"

It was unavoidable, they would find out soon enough, "I don't have parents. I live with my grandma."

"What about relatives? Uncle or an aunt?"

"I don't have any."

"How old are you?"

"Thirteen."

"Have you been living here alone since your grandma passed away?"

Henry took a deep breath. Hands fidget. "My grandma didn't die. She's in the hospital. The minister at church, he's going to help me."

"Well, until all that gets figured out, you can't stay here alone. We will have to take you to a youth home."

"What's that?"

"It's a home for kids your age. Kids who have lost their relatives go there until we can find homes for them."

"I don't need a home. I'm fine here with my grandma."

The lady seemed somewhat annoyed by Henry's talking. She walked around the room. "It's Henry, right?"

He had to repeat himself, "Yes, Henry Odin."

"Well, let's see if I can help you pack some things to take with you."

"No, I don't want to go, I can take care of myself, I'll be ok. The minister from church, he's going to help me."

"Thirteen is still too young to be left alone. You're a minor."

Henry fought back the tears as he said, "But I don't want to go."

"Well, where else can you go if you don't have relatives? Someone has to take care of you. We are going to take this house and sell it to someone else."

Henry buried his cries in his hands. "I just told you my grandma didn't die. She's in the hospital."

"You'll be fine. The people at the youth home will look after you."

At one point, the lady reached up to a shelf to touch a ceramic.

Henry pulled it out of her hand. "Don't touch

it. Grandma doesn't like it when people touch her things."

The lady made a face. "Look, we have little time, you need to decide what to take with you."

"I don't want to take anything with me. My grandma's coming back."

The lady crossed her arms. "Well, if you don't take anything with you right now, you will not see it again. We are going to sell it or give it away. Charities like all this old stuff. They like to give to people who can benefit from it."

Henry had no choice but to pack, so what should he pack? He couldn't take much in his backpack. He walked around the house, gathered his grandma's bible, her reading glasses along with her wallet and her red scarf. And then he noticed the set of candles sitting on her nightstand. He packed them up too.

Picked up his backpack. Stuffed his sorrows in his pockets and climbed into the back seat of the car. Took one last look at his grandma's house with the overgrown trees and the rocking chairs sitting on the porch and wondered if this too would soon become a fading memory just like his childhood. He took a deep breath, clenched his teeth, swallowed hard, and looked away.

The trip to the youth home was a short drive.

The car turned into a driveway leading up to a pretty yellow house with white windows.

Henry felt a sickening in his stomach. It was like reliving the past all over again. He walked through the front door, only to be ushered into a room he would share with another boy. He looked around. It, too, had the same sterile feeling as the children's home. The walls were void of any genuine character. The beds looked stiff; decorated with the most depressing colors he had ever seen—purple and grey. And to make matters worse, the room was missing a television.

He threw himself on the bed. Buried his face in the pillow, hoping no one could hear his muffled cries. The sorrows in his pockets began seeping out in broken pieces, to the point of suffocation. He coughed, trying to regain his breathing, when he felt a rush come up his throat. He leaned over the bed and puked on the floor.

Henry found himself alone again. Life was just not playing fair with him. It had deprived him of love the moment he had come into existence. And now it was on the verge of sucking away any bit of happiness he knew while living with his grandma. He needed a friend in his life to help him overcome this difficult time.

CHAPTER EIGHTEEN

Thursday, February 26, 1981 (Six days later)

Alvin Beard grabbed his coffee cup; picked up his toolbox and headed through the garden to fix the patio door. Along the way, he spotted a boy on a bench with a book over his face.

He stopped to take a sip from his cup, his eyes steady on the boy. He cleared his throat. "Hey, isn't it kind of early to be taking a nap?" He called out.

"Don't bother me."

"You should be out there playing with the other kids."

Henry mumbled under the book, "Leave me alone."

"Kids nowadays don't know how to go out and play anymore. All you want to do is sleep all day, talk on the phone with your friends all night. These are serious concerns."

Henry lifted the book from his face, sat up, and looked around. Alvin had settled on the back patio to sip the rest of his coffee and sort through his toolbox.

Henry shook his head, went back to lying on the bench.

Alvin fixed the latch on the patio door. Gathered all his tools and made his way back to where Henry was sitting.

"Hey, so what's your name?" Alvin asked.

Henry mumbled, "I don't know, and I don't care."

"You don't know your name?"

Annoyed because the man wasn't going away, Henry sat up and acknowledged him. "It's Henry."

"Henry what?"

"Doesn't matter."

"How long have you been staying here?"

Henry shrugged his shoulders, "Forever."

Alvin raised his eyebrows. "You've been here since you were a baby?"

Henry sighed, "It doesn't matter."

Alvin tipped his cap to scratch his head, "Hey, I was here not too long ago and I don't remember seeing you."

Henry lowered his head. "My grandma, she's in the hospital."

"I'm sorry. Is she going to be ok?"

"I think so."

"So, why are you here?"

"I can't stay home alone."

Alvin seemed interested. "Don't you have relatives?"

"Nah. It's just grandma and me."

"What about your mom?"

"I'm not supposed to be talking to strangers."

"So then, let's introduce ourselves. I'm Alvin Beard. I work in construction, but sometimes I help here with repairs when Frank, the maintenance guy, is out sick."

"Construction? What's that?"

"I build things and then when they break I put them back together, like today. I had to repair the door latch on the patio door. How long are you staying here?"

"I don't know."

Moments later, a tall brunette appeared through the back door. She had her hair pinned up. Small pair of reading glasses hung on a pretty chain around her neck. "Oh, here you are Mr. Beard. I have been looking all over for you." She said.

"Something else break?" Alvin replied.

"The restroom in the dining hall has a leaky faucet. Can you look at it before you leave?"

"On my way."

Alvin turned to Henry. "Get out there and play with the others. It will make you feel better."

CHAPTER NINETEEN

Tuesday, March 24, 1981 (A few weeks later)

A few weeks later, Alvin returned to the youth home to do another repair. Summoned to work a repair in the dining hall, he walked right in to find most of the kids sitting together having their lunch except for Henry, who was sitting alone by a corner window, pushing his food around with a fork.

Alvin wandered on over, "Why are you sitting by yourself?"

Silence.

"You should sit with some friends."

"I'm ok."

"So how's your grandma?"

"She's better."

Alvin's voice cracked. "I had a family member in the hospital too a few weeks ago. He didn't make it." He cleared his throat and took his ladder, positioned it under one of the light fixtures, "Hey Henry, since you're not eating, can you help me out for a moment? I need the screwdriver from my toolbox."

"What?"

"A screwdriver. It's in my toolbox."

Henry scratched his head. "What's that?"

"It's the long skinny tool with a pointed end and it has a yellow handle on it."

Henry sorted through the toolbox, sparking an interest in the variety of metal contraptions until he located the screwdriver. He turned to Alvin and asked, "What's all this?"

"Tools. My bare hands can't fix everything."

"What's this one? It has water in it."

"Yeah, that's a level. It helps me position things at a straight angle."

"What?"

"When I hang a picture on the wall, level helps me hang it straight. If you like, I can show you sometime."

"Nah."

"I tell you what, I'll talk to the director, see if she will give me permission to teach you a bit about how to repair things."

The director appeared through the doorway with a stack of folders in her arms. "Permission for what?"

Alvin turned around. "What do you think if Henry helps me with some of these repairs? Every time I come, he is doing nothing. This will teach him to become useful. He can also keep his mind busy. These days, an idle mind is not a good thing."

She gave Henry a smile. "Henry is going home this week. The minister at his church notified me grandma is getting out of the hospital. She is going to need him more than ever."

Henry's face lit up. "I'm going home? My grandma is coming to pick me up?"

"Your grandma's church is sending over one of their ministers to pick you up."

"When?"

"Friday." She said.

Alvin chimed in, "That is great to hear, but how about I just teach him a bit, anyway? I'll be here all this week. I think it'll be good for Henry to learn how these tools work, never know when he might have to fix his own stuff."

She removed her eyeglasses; "Henry, do you think you would be interested in helping Mr. Beard for a few days?"

Henry shrugged his shoulders, "I guess so."

With his easy and genuine character, Alvin would soon become the friend Henry needed in his life at that moment.

That week, Henry took delight in seeing Alvin come around because it not only meant he would get to help with some sort of repair, but it also meant he could enjoy lunch in the garden with him instead of eating in a noisy dining hall. He especially liked to just sit and listen to Alvin's stories. Sometimes, though, the stories seemed to be farfetched, yet it was okay with

Henry, because it felt good to sit and escape his present situation.

At the end of the week, Henry said his goodbyes to the youth home and to Alvin. He felt grateful for the time spent there. Not only were the people kind, but they also helped him to manage his anxiety when he was struggling with being away from his grandma.

Chapter Twenty

I returned to grandma's house to find the peace and love I knew so well. It was the only place in the world I could call home. Grandma had taken me in and given me the home I never had with my mom. We always kept busy with chores around the house. She made sure we had enough food on the table at all times, even if it meant having to ask for help from her church. Over the years, she taught me about being kind to others. She taught me to never give up when things get hard, like in school. And she taught me about how God is there for me every day, in my good days and even when I am at my worst. All I need to do is reach out to him and ask for help.

Grandma hasn't been able to get back to her old self since returning from the hospital. She can't walk too far because she gets tired fast. She forgets where she put things. Sometimes she even forgets what day it is. Seeing her like this scares me.

I've had to buckle up and be a man, just like my mom used to tell me. Seeing how grandma can't move around the house much these days, the chores are now mine to do. I mop, sweep. I even learned how to cook some of grandma's delicious recipes. Grandma says I don't use enough salt, but I think that's good because she doesn't have to worry about her feet swelling up so much. I learned how to mow the yard and make it look pretty. Grandma says we can win the best yard prize around the neighborhood if I keep it up.

And even though grandma can't drive anymore, we still get to church three times a week thanks to one of her friends who gives us a ride.

As the years have gone by, I still sit by the window and think about my mom. Haven't given up hope. I know she's out there somewhere, wish I could find her. Been thinking about grandma's car. It's been sitting there for a long time, getting old and rusty. One day last week while grandma was sleeping, I snuck the keys from her purse and started the car with no problem. It felt good to get behind the wheel of such a fine old car. I moved it back and forth in the driveway. This week I've even taken it around the block to see how it feels on the road. It drives well. I know to stop at all the stop signs too. Maybe one day I can drive grandma and me to my graduation.

CHAPTER TWENTY-ONE

Friday, May 23, 1986 (Five years later)

Henry found himself deep in thought over the details of his high school graduation. Could he drive himself to the auditorium? How many people would be in attendance? Would he find his friends? Then he shifted his thoughts back to his grandma. His hope had always been to have her at his graduation. Her heart condition wasn't allowing her to be very mobile anymore. He offered to take her in a wheelchair, but she refused. She felt happy just to have Henry's graduation photo by her bedside. She assured Henry she would be okay not going.

Henry took one last look in the mirror. Licked his finger, padded down his patch of blond hair. The blue tie needed a little more fixing. He dusted off his navy blue slacks, wiped a mark off his shiny shoes. Walked into the living room with a smile.

Grandma was sitting in her rocker, waiting. Her tired eyes lit up when she saw him. "Henry, you look very handsome. If your mom were here today, I think she would be very proud of you, too. I thank God every day for the help he has brought me over the years. With his help, I've been able to raise you to be a good man. I need to be praying he provides a way for you to go to college. And if not, maybe a good job."

"Yeah grandma. I need to graduate first, then I'll think about that other stuff."

"Where's your cap and gown? Can't forget that. We paid some good money for all that."

Henry gave his grandma a peck on the cheek and went on his way to his ceremony.

Town people always took great pride in their youth. They considered high school an outstanding achievement in the small community. It was no surprise then when they decorated the auditorium with everything from streamers to balloons and banners. Henry took his seat close to the stage. He could feel his anxiety stirring up on the inside. Perhaps it was from so much excitement. Take a deep breath. Take a deep breath. All these years, he still couldn't get used to being around sizeable crowds with so much noise. Friends and family gathered around the auditorium, waiting for the ceremony to start so they could see the graduates cross the stage. Henry scanned the crowded room, looking for someone he might know.

There was no one. His school friends had not yet arrived. He kept his eyes on the stage. Thinking about his future and what it might bring. He also thought about his mom. What would she think if she were here? Would she be proud of him like these other parents? A tap on the shoulder interrupted his thoughts. He turned around.

"Henry, is that you?" She asked.

I looked at the stranger in front of me. Was I supposed to know who she was? Should I even ask?

"Henry, I'm Mary Ann. Remember me? From the children's home?"

I stood up and hugged her. Mary Ann! How could I forget her? Had it not been for her help during my early childhood years, no telling where I might be today. I remember wishing my mom could be more like her.

"Henry, I'm so proud of you. You look good." She said.

"My grandma..."

"Yes, your grandma has taken good care of you. She called to tell me about your graduation a few days ago. I had to come see you. What do you plan to do after graduation? Are you going to college?"

"Grandma wants me to try community college first. See if I like it. If not, I'll get a job."

"College will be good for you, Henry. There you can learn anything you want."

"I think I want to work with my hands."

"You mean like build stuff?"

"Yes. I took a woodworking shop class in school."

"How about your mom, Henry? Did she ever come back?"

"No, but grandma prays for her every day."

"That's good. And how are you doing with your anxiety?"

"Better. At school, I have a therapist who helps me."

Mary Ann and Henry continued their conversation for a little longer before she gave Henry another hug. A sign she was getting ready to leave. She pulled back a moment and said, "I almost forgot. I got you something."

Henry's eyes lit up.

Mary Ann handed him a small box wrapped in blue paper. "If I should not get to see you later, here is a little something for you. Open it when you get home."

Hours later, after all the celebration stuff had calmed down, Henry was back home in his room, relieved to close this chapter of his life. Sitting on his bed, he remembered the small box Mary Ann had given him at the graduation. She'd gifted him a brown leather wallet that was the perfect size for his pockets. He flipped it open to find a note and a hundred-dollar bill. The note read:

Henry,

I am so proud of the man you've become. I wish you a life filled with all the happiness in the world. You deserve it. Take this scripture and hold it close to your heart always. Psalm 51:10-12.

Henry wiped his teary eyes, buried his face in the pillow. He felt fear settling in right next to him, just like when he was a kid back in the day when his mom would leave him alone in the apartment. He was afraid of what the future was going to bring him. Would he be ok out in the world without grandma? What kind of job would he get? Would he make some new friends? Too many questions running through his mind, it was all making him feel anxious. Take a deep breath. Take a deep breath. Be brave. Be brave. Brave is good. Being brave can help me.

CHAPTER TWENTY-TWO

Wednesday, August 27, 1986

I took Grandma to the hospital a few weeks before I was to start college. This time, she never returned home. I think she held on as long as she could over the summer so I could have a place to live while we waited for college to start. Looking back on those days, I know why she was eager to get rid of her stuff. We kept having garage sale after garage sale. She saved every penny and then gave it all to me. Telling me it would come in handy when I went off to college. She knew what was coming ahead.

I walked through the empty house one last time. Taking in her lingering scent. Trying to preserve every precious memory I'd made with grandma by my side.

I wiped my tears one last time. Picked up my bags. Walked away. This time, I didn't look back. My heart was at peace. It was time to embark on the next chapter of my life.

CHAPTER TWENTY-THREE

Saturday, September 6, 1986

The community college didn't have but four two-story buildings. Two student living buildings were at the back end of the campus. Those buildings were a bit more intimidating. Tall and skinny with so many windows, I imagined what an evening with thunderstorms might feel like. Must admit, for an eighteen-year-old boy, I felt scared. I no longer had grandma to give me advice or to help me whenever I'd get in a pickle over something stupid. I was alone. Take a deep breath. Take a deep breath. What I needed was to make some new friends. My high school friends disappeared after graduation, taking jobs out of town. They were ready to leave family and everyone behind, including me. I swallowed hard.

CHAPTER TWENTY-FOUR

Thursday, October 23, 1986
(Over a month later)

I had no problem adjusting to college life, partly because I had a roommate. New to campus, we hung out together and attended several activities, hoping to meet some new people. It was much easier for him, though. He didn't have the anxiety issues I did. There were times I had to withdraw from social events because of the noise level or the crowds. I didn't give up; I kept trying.

The class instruction was at a much faster pace than in high school. I tried to keep up by attending tutoring sessions. And today was going to be even more challenging. Studying for the midterm algebra test. Feeling anxious, I couldn't get myself to focus. I shoved everything to the side and headed to the gym to see if some form of exercise might help me relax.

Midway to the gym, I heard a voice from behind me, "Hey, you're Henry, right?"

I turned around. "Do I know you?" I asked.

"We're in the same English class, you doing ok? Do you need any help?"

"English class is fine. It's the algebra I'm struggling with. I scheduled some tutoring in the math lab."

"What are you doing tonight? Want to go to a party?"

"I, no, I need to study so I can pass this class."

"Yeah, ok. If you change your mind, here's a flyer. I'll be there with some other friends."

I looked at the flyer. Stuffed it in my pocket. Continued on my way to the gym. The party idea seemed of interest. Perhaps I could attend at another time. Right now, I needed to exercise all my anxiety away and get back to studying for my test so I could get through this first year of college.

CHAPTER TWENTY-FIVE

Thursday, March 17, 1988 (A year later)

College was proving to be quite a challenge for me. It had become much more work than I ever expected, still I had completed my first year. I was so proud of myself. I accomplished something on my own without grandma. And here I was now, pushing through my second year of school. The pressures of late night studying were taking a toll. Not getting enough sleep. My eating habits were all over the place. I needed an outlet, a release of some sort. The end of the week was here. I considered catching up on my sleep, but dismissed the idea when I heard an abrupt knock on the door.

"Henry, hey open the door."

I pulled the door open.

"Henry, I'm passing out flyers. We're having a party downstairs. You and your roommate should come."

"I don't know. I'll ask my roommate to see if he wants to go."

"Come on Henry, you need to get out of your

room and come hang out with us for a bit. We're having food, drinks and watching a movie. It'll be fun, you'll see."

I tossed the flyer in the trash. A few minutes later, I pulled it out and looked at it. Invited many times to other parties and always I ignored the invitations, yet this time I felt the inkling to go out and loosen up. Left my roommate a note. Grabbed my sweatshirt, shoes and headed downstairs. Figured the party included a few of the other students in the building. My plan was to go hang out a bit and most likely be back at my apartment within an hour.

Upon seeing the sizeable crowd, I began feeling anxious, and a bit suffocated too. I pulled back a moment. Take a deep breath. Take a deep breath. Some guests were having deep conversations in one area, while others watched a movie. I continued moving throughout the room. At one point, I waved to some familiar faces as I made my way to the table with the delicious treats. Having not eaten much all day, it felt good to eat something else besides cold noodles and beans.

Within minutes, I found myself a comfortable seat by the window, hoping to enjoy the party from a distance with no interactions or conversations with others. The plan was to sit and breathe. I soon abandoned the plan when the host caught sight of me and came around to join me.

He asked, "You like the party?"

"Yeah, it's good to get out of the room." I said.

"I have an extra beer. Here you want one?"

I pulled back, "No, I don't drink."

"What do you mean you don't drink, Henry? Everyone drinks these days. Here, take it. It's still cold. One beer won't hurt you."

Henry took the beer, held it in his hand and then placed it on the window seal. He felt hesitant to take a sip, yet everyone else in the room seemed like they were having fun drinking. Maybe it was best if he took a few sips to fit in with the crowd. He drank the entire beer. Some time later, he felt an uneasy feeling in his stomach, in his head and in his throat. He couldn't determine if the uneasy feeling was because of the food or the beer. Maybe it was a mix of the two. Either way, he headed back to his apartment. Feeling what was about to happen, he placed his hand over his mouth. Raced to the bathroom just in time. Never had he felt so ill after attending a party. But then he had never attended a party like this. In fact, this was his first experience with alcohol and it sure wasn't a pleasant one.

Chapter Twenty-Six

Months later.

The party experience had left a sour taste in my mouth. After the drinking incident, I brushed off all invitations. Turned my focus to finishing up my last semester. I also got to thinking about what I was going to do with the rest of my life and where I was going to live. Had no job prospects. The job fair wasn't much help, either. Most of the companies were looking for students to work in the financial industry or in business. I had no desire to sit on a stool and count money for people all day, nor did I have an interest in working in an office. From what I had heard about office work, it involved sitting in a small cubicle for eight hours typing lengthy reports of some sort. Someone sitting in a big corner office with glass windows monitored employee lunches and restroom breaks all day long. Pushed those thoughts out of my mind and turned my attention to packing my stuff. I was ready to do something else besides school.

With two years of school behind me, it should be enough to get me a decent job.

Henry and his roommate spent the final days cleaning and rearranging the apartment back to its original form so the school could grant them official transfer status or, in Henry's case, program completion.

"Henry, what are your plans after school?" The roommate asked.

Henry's voice cracked. "Well, now that my grandma is gone, I don't have a home to go to. The youth home where I spent some time when I was thirteen only takes teenagers up to the age of eighteen. I'm not sure what to do right now."

His roommate's eyes lit up. "Hey you can come back with me to Georgia. My mom and dad won't mind. We have plenty of space."

"No thanks, I think I'll stay here in the city."

"Maybe I can help you find a place."

Henry shrugged, "Like where? I don't have a job, and without a job, I can't get an apartment."

Roommate looked around the room. "I thought I saw a phone book around here somewhere. Let's see what we can find in it."

Several phone calls later, Henry's roommate located a shelter blocks away from the college.

Just like that. Henry decided he would move into a family shelter. The nauseating feeling deep in the pit of his stomach had returned.

He wanted to throw up. What other choices did he have at the moment? None. The thought of sleeping in his car crossed his mind, but then quickly dismissed it. And his roommate, well, he didn't enjoy being away from home, so he headed back home to Georgia to finish his final two years of college.

CHAPTER TWENTY-SEVEN

Wednesday, May 11, 1988

P eople walking through the busy intersection seemed driven with a purpose of pushing ahead in their storied lives. They had places to go, people to see, things to do. Henry just stood there in silence. He had no purpose; no actual story, just some disconnected pieces of memories he had collected over the years and two bags of belongings. He let go of his meaningless thoughts and turned around to look at the lifeless building in front of him, which was tall and very grey. There were no flowers, no trees, and not even a pretty wooden door, or a welcome mat, just a sterile glass door. It lacked all the character and warmth of a home. He picked up his bags, walked inside only to find the interior wasn't much different. The smell of fresh paint was overwhelming. Fake plants gave the lobby a sterile feeling while a few yellow chairs occupied the rest of the space.

He provided the required personal information to a young woman at the front desk and, soon thereafter, found himself being escorted through an endless maze of hallways to get to his assigned room.

Any kind of hope for his life diminished the moment she pushed open the door. The sunlight filtering through the small window wasn't enough to cheer the depressing shade of grey on the walls. The built-in shelving unit looked as if it might be more suitable for a prison cell. A cot on the opposite side looked a bit worn. And the only other pieces of furniture in the room were two folding chairs and a small table. He shook his head in disbelief. His present situation looked dire. At that moment, he felt like a fool for not having shown more interest in the offerings at the job fair. Right about now, an office job and a pretty apartment overlooking the city lights sure seemed more inviting than this place. Anxiety and fear were always to blame for trying to hinder his progress in life. He had to learn to think for himself, learn how to maneuver life through society so he could take control of his situation, otherwise he might end up on the street.

Hours later.

The knock on the door forced Henry to pull himself together. He wiped his eyes.

The young woman spoke first. "Mr. Odin,

there are a few construction sites hiring in the area."

Henry looked at the woman. "What?"

"Mr. Odin, you said you had some experience with wood work so we put together a list of jobs for you."

"Oh yes, I know a little, but I don't think I can..."

"In order for you to remain here at the shelter, you must go out and look for work."

"Yes, but..."

"The addresses are on this paper. Go see them tomorrow."

She handed him the paper and disappeared back into the maze of hallways.

Henry let out a deep sigh of frustration. Construction? He knew nothing about working on a construction site. He knew about working with the hammer and other tools, but only in a woodworking shop setting. His interest was in creating wooden sculptures. He kicked the chair over, smoothed back his hair.

Thursday, May 12, 1988 (The following day)

For Henry, his lack of experience mattered little because the construction foreman at the first site needed help, so he hired him on the spot.

Thanks to grandma and all her years of

pushing Henry to be an early riser, he would have no trouble getting to work on time. He made sure his headphones were with him at all times, too. They helped keep the noise level down. End of the first week, Henry earned his first paycheck.

"Henry, here's your paycheck."

He peeked inside the envelope and smiled.

The foreman asked him, "What are you going to do with your first paycheck?"

"I'm going to buy more tools."

"You like the job?"

"Yeah, working with my hands is good. I prefer to work in the woodworking shop, but this is okay for now."

"You can work more hours. Save the extra money, so one day you can set up your woodworking shop."

Henry's eyes lit up, "Sure."

"Then show up on Saturday. We can always use an extra hand."

"Ok."

CHAPTER TWENTY-EIGHT

At twenty-five-years-old, Henry was finally showing signs of responsibility. Steady employment had paved a way for him to move out of the family shelter and into a small apartment. It had also given him the means to fix grandma's old car and keep it running for a little longer. He was on track to have a suitable life when, out of nowhere, a trap appeared.

"Hey Henry, we are all going to have a drink after work at the bar around the corner. Why don't you come with us?"

"Nah, I'm tired. I'm going home." Henry replied.

"It's Sam's birthday. You can't miss it."

Henry tipped his cap, scratched his head, "Yeah, ok, I can come for a little while."

The co-worker put his arm around Henry, "See you soon."

Before meeting up with the guys after work,

Henry made a quick stop at the icehouse. Picked up a newspaper and sorted through all the ads, looking for used items for his apartment before moving onto the obituary section. It had become part of his daily routine for the last few years. He searched the names; the pictures one by one, hoping something would surface regarding his mother. Nothing. He shoved the paper aside. Would try again tomorrow. Right now, he needed to go join the others around the corner.

The bar had the look of an old weathered barn. The laughter and the loudness of the music seemed a bit much for Henry. Take a deep breath. Take a deep breath. He felt uncomfortable. The drinking incident in college had left him scared. And now here he was. He promised himself he would only have one beer and then be on his way home. The guys had other plans.

"Here Henry, I've got a cold beer for you."

Henry hesitated at first, but then picked up the bottle and held it in his hand, contemplating whether to drink it or put it back on the counter and walk right back out the door. As he looked around the room, everyone seemed to be having a good time by the way they were laughing and enjoying each other's company. He, too, wanted to be a part of all the fun; otherwise, he would find himself alone for good. Tired of being alone. Girlfriends never hung around for more than a month. If only to have friends to hang out with, maybe play some poker or go fishing. His attention turned back to the bottle in hand. Maybe if he just drank one beer, it would be ok and he could still hang out and engage in conversation. He took a sip. The taste was refreshing and perfect after a long day out in the sun.

"You like it?" One guy asked.

"Yeah, it's good."

"Okay then, let's get you another one."

"No, I have to be leaving."

"You have to drink this one, too. I paid for it."

Not wanting to create an argument of sorts with the co-worker, he accepted the beer.

Wednesday, November 3, 1993
(The following day)

Henry arrived late for work.

The foreman called him out, "Henry, where have you been?"

"Went out with the guys to drink. Overslept. I'm sorry."

"Don't let it happen again. After the third time, we let you go. We lose money if we don't stay on schedule to finish the project. And when we lose money, people lose their jobs. Get it?"

Henry dusted off his cap. "Yeah, okay."

CHAPTER TWENTY-NINE

Friday, November 12, 1993
(A couple of weeks later)

The stresses of working long hours six days a week and trying to fit in socializing with the guys after work were proving to be a challenge for twenty-five-year-old Henry. He had exchanged the favor of God for some senseless loyalty to a group of guys who had no regard for God or anything in relation.

Tonight's evening out on the town had left him more disoriented than usual, causing him to trip on a step as he made his way up the flight of stairs to the apartment building where he lived. Upon reaching the door, his key failed to fit into the key slot. He tried over and over but kept failing. At one point, he kicked the door loud enough to alert other tenants in the building.

The neighboring door across the hallway flew open, a man shouted, "Hey, you're waking everyone up! I'm calling security!"

Minutes later security arrived to find Henry

at the bottom of the staircase holding on to the rail.

"Mr. Odin, you lost again? This is the third time we have to come out to help you. Come on, let's go find your apartment."

Henry got to his apartment, only to find a notice posted at the door.

"What's this?" He asked security.

"Mr. Odin, it's an eviction notice."

"For being a few weeks late? What do I do now? All my stuff is in there."

"I'm sorry, Mr. Odin, I can't open the door."

Henry launched himself at the door, kicking and yelling.

"Mr. Odin, I'm going to have to ask you to leave."

"No, I need my stuff. How am I supposed to go to work tomorrow? I need to shower and change clothes."

"Tomorrow you can go talk to Roxanne at the office. Right now, I need you to get in your car and see if you can calm yourself down, or else..."

Henry shouted back, "Or else what? What? What are you going to do?"

"I'll have to call the police to have you re-moved from the premises. We will also tow your vehicle away."

Henry stumbled into his car, trying to make sense of what was happening to him. He shouted,

"This is wrong! I need my stuff!" He wanted to go back upstairs, bust the window, and pull all his things out. That type of action would most likely land him in jail. He quickly dismissed the idea. He laid his head on the steering wheel. It was no use battling something he had no control over. Tonight he was better off sleeping in his car. He took off his cap. Pulled off the work boots, and closed his eyes.

CHAPTER THIRTY

Saturday, November 13, 1993
(The following day)

The sound of cars driving through the parking lot, kids playing with a soccer ball and a baby crying in the background was enough noise to wake Henry from his deep sleep. No idea of the hour, but judging by the way the sun was glaring in his face; it had to be way past seven. He needed to get to work, but first he had to do something about his appearance. He headed to the nearest gas station to find a restroom to get cleaned up and buy some chewing gum.

The foreman looked at his watch. "Henry, you showed up. You're two hours late. What happened to you this time, Henry?"

"Slept in my car last night because I got locked out of my apartment."

"This is the third time in two weeks you show up late. Robert is taking over your job today. We can't wait on you, Henry."

"Sorry." Henry whispered.

"Sorry isn't enough anymore. Look at you; you're wearing the same clothes you had on yesterday. And what's with that odor? Henry, no one wants to work with you when you show up like this."

"I didn't have any clothes to change into."

"Are you doing drugs?"

"Nah, it's nothing like that."

The foreman eyed him. "What is it, Henry? The drinking?"

"No, I go out with friends and sometimes lose track of time, then I end up getting to bed late. For some reason I don't hear the alarm. It won't happen again, I promise."

The foreman turned away. "I'm sorry Henry, I'm going to have to let you go."

"No, no, I need this job! Please, just give me another chance. I got an eviction notice last night. I need to work to pay rent."

"No Henry. You've had three warnings. We don't have the time to listen to all your excuses. We are running a project around here. Go get your stuff together. Security will escort you out the gate. Oh, and you can pickup your last paycheck next Friday."

Henry whispered something underneath his breath, gathered his tools and got in his car. He looked out the window. All the other guys were busy working. They all knew how to handle their stories. And him, he was always having trouble with his story. It just seemed to be an ongoing battle to get ahead in life. He hit the steering wheel, started his car, and drove off.

An hour later.

Henry was back at the apartment complex arguing his situation and trying to find a way to get back into his apartment.

"I'm sorry, Mr. Odin, you are required to pay on a weekly basis for your apartment. Our records show you are behind on the rent by three weeks now. If you pay today, we open the apartment for you."

"I don't have the money right now!" Henry yelled.

"Mr. Odin, we can't wait on you any longer."

"Can I have my clothes?"

"I'm sorry."

"Please, I need some clean clothes."

"Mr. Odin, we will have a garage sale to recoup some of the rent money you owe us."

"No, no, you can't do that!"

"It was all in the agreement you signed."

Henry's voice cracked. "My grandma's things are in there too."

The lady made a face. "I tell you what; we are having a garage sale on the last Saturday of the month. If you can get here by eight, you can buy back your grandma's things and anything else you want."

"Are you serious? You're going to make me buy my own stuff? How stupid is that?"

"We sell to the public at nine."

At that point, Henry turned around; kicked a chair over and slammed the door behind him.

He felt doomed. His livelihood was in that apartment. If he wanted to keep it, he would have to buy it back. The past was always coming back into his present to keep him from succeeding in life. The anger in him needed to be soothed with a cold beer. Unfortunately, all he had to his name right now was a crumpled twenty-dollar bill. He kicked the trash bag over the curb as he made his way back to the car to think about where he was going to get his next shower and a good night's sleep so he could figure out his situation. A place came to mind.

Same day mid afternoon.

Henry entered the building. Not much had changed in décor over the last five years. The reception desk looked the same, too.

"Hello, how can we help you?"

"I need a place to stay. I lost my apartment."

"For how long?"

"I don't know. I lost my job today too."

"Have you been here before?"

Henry sighed in frustration, "Yeah, it's been a while. I think maybe about five years."

"We've updated our system. You may have to fill out forms again. Your name, please."

"Henry Odin."

"Looks like we have some of your information in our old files. Are we adding family to your file too?"

"No, just me."

"Do you still work in construction?"

"Yeah."

"Here, take this. It's our list of jobs in the area. There are a few construction jobs in there, too."

Overcome with emotion, Henry covered his face.

"Mr. Odin, it's going to be ok, we are here to help you. We get many people passing through here with nothing but the clothes on their backs. I was homeless until a year ago. If I had not found this place, no telling where I'd be today. This place saved me."

Henry wiped his face.

The receptionist continued, "We have only a few beds available in the shared rooms. Are you ok with that?"

"That's fine."

"Did you bring anything with you?"

"Just what I have on. They wouldn't let me take anything out of my apartment."

The receptionist motioned. "There's a clothing

room at the end of the last hallway. Volunteers will help you find whatever you need. We get clothes almost every week from some very generous people. We even have a chef who volunteers two days out of the week to cook in the kitchen. He works at one of those fancy restaurants. I'm in love with the turkey sandwiches he makes. He will be here tomorrow."

Feeling the tension, Henry rubbed the back of his neck and said, "Oh, I almost forgot to ask. Do you have any candles?"

The receptionist looked at him suspiciously.

Henry corrected his request; "I light a candle for my mother every night."

"What happened to her?"

"She disappeared when I was young."

"Sorry to hear that. I'll get you one from the kitchen."

"Thank you."

By evening time Henry had settled into his shared room. Disconnected thoughts were cluttering his mind. He wanted desperately to piece them together. Maybe then his mind would be free of anxiety and fear would leave him alone once and for all. Take a deep breath. Take a deep breath. He shifted his focus to the list of jobs and then shoved it aside. Looked around the room. Feeling grateful the family shelter existed. He choked back his tears. Pulled the string on the lamp and closed his eyes.

CHAPTER THIRTY-ONE

Monday, November 15, 1993 (Two days later)

When Monday morning came around, Henry wasted no time in looking for a job. He inquired at multiple sites, only to be told there were no openings. He looked at the list again. One last opportunity, maybe he would have better luck.

The foreman asked, "Do you have any experience?"

"Yes."

"Fill out this application. We will call you."

Henry tipped his cap, scratched his head in discouragement, and filled out the application anyway. With no phone number to give, he would have to use the shelter's number; otherwise they could never find him.

All hope of finding a job had come to an end by late afternoon. He felt defeated, as he headed back to the shelter. Parked and sat in his car when he noticed a help wanted sign at the site across the street. Late in the day, he contemplated whether he should just skip it. He took a deep breath. Put his baseball cap on one more time and said, "All they can tell me is no."

He knocked on the trailer door. "Yeah, it's open," a voice called out.

Henry opened the door.

"Come in, I'm on the phone."

Henry stood by the door.

After some minutes, the man hung the phone up. "Can I help you with something?" He asked.

Henry stuttered, "I'm, I'm here about the help wanted sign."

"Oh yeah, so what can you do?"

"Frame, sheetrock and paint. I've installed some flooring, too."

"Do you know anything about plumbing, air conditioning, or electrical wiring?"

"I know how it all works."

"How much experience?"

"About five years."

"Do you have your own tools?"

"Yes."

"Okay then, fill out this application."

"Do you want me to bring it back tomorrow?" Henry asked.

"No, you can fill it out right now. Use the picnic table outside."

"Ok."

A while later, Henry returned to the trailer with the application in hand.

"All done?"

"Yes."

The man pulled out a chair. "Here sit down." He said.

The man studied the application, cleared his throat, and then studied Henry.

Henry kept his hands steady on his baseball cap trying not to get anxious.

"Henry Odin? I remember you. You're that kid from the youth home. What have you been up to?"

"Community college for a couple of years."

"What did you study?"

"Got into woodworking."

"What kind of stuff did you make?"

"Wood sculptures."

The foreman crossed his arms. "Why are you here?"

"I need a job."

"What happened to your last job?"

"It didn't work out."

"So you married? Kids?"

"Nah."

"I'm sorry. I didn't mean to get you all teary-eyed." Alvin Beard picked up the napkins sitting on his desk and passed them on to Henry. "Okay, so tomorrow can you be here at seven?"

"Yes."

"You're hired."

"Thank you."

"Oh, and one last thing."

Henry put his baseball cap on.

"I run a tight schedule. Everyone has to be here by 6:30. I like to have meetings with the guys about any issues before we start for the day." Alvin took his cap and stood up. "And I don't tolerate people coming in late."

Henry nodded, turned around and walked back across the street to the shelter, feeling grateful. Somehow, someway, God had opened a door for him.

The receptionist greeted him in the lobby, "Hi Mr. Odin, did you have any luck with any of the jobs on the list?"

"No, but the site across the street had a help wanted sign. The foreman hired me on the spot. I start tomorrow."

"That's great news."

"Yeah, I'm feeling good about it."

"Have you had anything to eat today?"

"No."

"The dining room is serving dinner in about thirty minutes. Get there on time because we run out of food fast."

For that reason, he showed up at the cafeteria right on time. Wanted to sit down and eat like everyone else. The noise level coming from the many conversations around the room was too much for Henry's anxiety. He took his tray of food to his room to be alone with his thoughts so he could think about the direction his life needed to take. If only mom had been more caring and more loving, would he be in this position right now? Would he still be living at home with her? He made a face. Pushed the thoughts aside.

Soon thereafter, his roommate appeared through the doorway. "Hey, you missed the dinner. It was pretty good." He said.

"I ate in here."

The roommate launched himself on the cot next to Henry. "I sure could use a beer right now."

The same idea had crossed Henry's mind for most of the day, yet he had dismissed it, understanding he needed to find a job.

The roommate continued, "You think if we went and got a few beers they would be ok with it?"

Henry made a face, "I have to be up early tomorrow. I start a new job."

CHAPTER THIRTY-TWO

Tuesday, November 16, 1993
(The following day)

Early the next morning, Henry arrived at work on foot. Alvin felt the need to ask him about his transportation, but decided he would leave it for another time.

"Henry, there's a pot of coffee over by the trailer. Help yourself."

"Nah, I'm fine."

"Ok then, let's get you started. Everyone around here works in teams of two. You'll be working with one of my best men, Albert."

Henry tipped his cap, "Ok."

Alvin added, "Albert will get you started with the framing on building one."

Henry nodded as he followed Albert to the designated building. By mid morning, their team had completed most of the required framing. The work was fast-paced and a bit much for Henry, but he stayed with it. The headphones over his ears helped reduce much of the sounds around, which made it easier for him to stay focused and keep up with Albert at all times.

Five hours later.

Albert asked Henry, "Where's your lunch?"

"I, well, don't eat lunch."

Albert laughed. "You're like the first guy I know who passes up lunch."

Alvin stepped out of his trailer to talk to the crew. Noticed Henry sitting in the shade with his cap over his face. He called out to him, "You're not eating lunch?"

"Nah, I'm ok."

"Well, if you're not eating, you need to drink water. The days are long around here. Go get some water from the jug. I don't want to call E.M.S. on your first day."

At the close of the day, Henry kept his distance from the crew for fear he might get invited to drink. He dusted his cap off, picked up his tools and took off on foot to the shelter across the street.

Alvin watched as Henry disappeared into the building. He asked the guys, "Hey any of you know what the building across the street is?"

One guy responded, "Oh, I think it's one of those family shelters."

Alvin couldn't believe after all Henry had been through as a kid, he was still struggling. He wondered what had gone wrong in Henry's life. Perhaps there was a way he could find out.

CHAPTER THIRTY-THREE

Wednesday, November 17, 1993
(The following day)

As the workday came to a close, Alvin took Henry aside. "You have a moment?"

"Yes."

"Let's go inside the trailer."

Henry took off his cap and sat down.

"Why are you staying at the family shelter across the street?"

Henry took a deep breath. "I got kicked out of my weekly apartment."

"What happened?"

"One night I went to get in. They had changed the locks on me. Couldn't get any of my stuff out. Ended up sleeping in my car that night. The next day, I checked into the shelter again."

Alvin looked puzzled. "What do you mean again?"

"After college, I didn't know what I was going to do. My college roommate helped me find the family shelter. It's not an awful place. They provide food and clothing. They even help people find jobs."

"Where's your car?"

"It's parked at the shelter."

Henry took a deep breath. He could feel his hands sweating. The conversation was becoming stressful. Take a deep breath. Take a deep breath. Alvin just kept bombarding him with questions. What interest did he have in his life, anyway? It's not like they were long-lost buddies and needed to catch up. They hardly knew each other. The man had been gracious enough to hire him on the spot. Henry felt the least he could do was sit and have a talk with him.

Alvin wanted to know more about Henry's life. He continued, "I don't mean to pry. I'm interested to know why you would lose your apartment if you were paying by the week? Are you involved in drugs?"

"No."

"Then what?"

"Drinking. Having a hard time, lately I spend all my money on drinking."

"And right now, how do you feel?"

"Feel like I want to crash. Want to drink my days and nights so I don't have to feel or think. Good thing is I don't have a dime right now. Spent the last of my money on gas to find a job." Henry wiped his face. "Can't seem to get ahead in anything. The moment things go well for me, something happens."

Alvin sat back in his chair, crossed his arms, and eyed Henry for a moment.

Henry gave him a frown. "What?"

"I'm thinking you should come stay at my house."

Henry stood up, "Nah, I'll be ok." He put his cap back on. "I'm used to being on my own."

Alvin wouldn't take no for an answer. He persisted, "I think it would be a lot better than the family shelter. I could help you get into a program at church. Help you get your life back on track."

"Appreciate you wanting to help, but I'll figure it out. Always do." He walked to the door, grabbed the doorknob.

"No Henry, let me lock up here and we'll go get your car and you follow me home."

CHAPTER THIRTY-FOUR

Alvin Beard's home was a distance away. In fact, he lived in a small community outside the city. An affluent neighborhood not too far from where I had lived, with grandma. We drove through well manicured streets to get to his home. Couldn't help but admire the homes. Each one looked unique in design. There was no doubt the builder had created the neighborhood with families in mind. Along the way, I spotted tennis courts, a swimming pool, and even a playground. The scenic pictures provided a glimpse of family life at its finest. Kept my eyes on the road for the rest of the drive. Followed Alvin into a long driveway of a charming brick house with black shutters and white trim windows. The large front porch appeared to be in the final stages of renovation.

No sooner did Alvin open his door did the front door to the home burst open. "Grandpa!" Alvin gathered his young grandson in his arms. "How was school today?" He asked.

"The teacher said my reading was good. I can be her helper tomorrow."

"Very good." Alvin planted a kiss on his

grandson's cheek. "Henry, this is my grandson, Jonah. Let's go inside so you can meet my wife, too."

The delicious aroma of food made me hungry the moment I entered the home. It brought back memories of when grandma used to cook. My attention then shifted to the interior of the home. There was a sense of warmth and love on full display. Neatly arranged family photos on a wall in the living room seemed a pleasant touch. Scattered on a rug in front of the television were several toys and books. An old bible sat on a small coffee table. A floral arrangement on the kitchen table even added an extra touch of love. It was clear Alvin's home had real heart. I on the other hand had none. I suppressed my emotions, hoping no one would notice.

A petite woman came up to Alvin. She greeted him with a kiss.

"Henry, this is my wife, Jeanie."

She extended her hand. "I'm so glad to meet you, Henry."

Alvin added, "Henry's been staying at the shelter across from the job site. I was thinking we could help him get back on track."

Jeanie's eyes lit up. "Oh yes, we have a spare room. After dinner, I can get it ready for you."

"Don't go change anything for me, I can sleep anywhere."

Alvin hugged Henry. "We are going to help you, son."

Henry's eyes teared up again. Not since Mary Ann or his grandma had anyone shown any regard for his wellbeing until today. There was the youth home; the shelter, but they didn't have the same effect.

Jonah interrupted, "Grandpa, I helped grandma make dinner."

"It's smells delicious. I'm sure Henry is starving, don't think he's had much to eat today."

"Grandpa, can I say the prayer at dinner?"

"Yes, you can."

Jonah began, "Thank you, God, for my mommy, my grandpa and my grandma. And thank you God for the food we eat, and for my new puppy I want. Amen."

Henry winked at Jonah.

Alvin burst out laughing, "Jonah, did I hear you say new puppy?"

"Grandpa, the neighbor wants to give me a puppy for Christmas. Please, can I have one? Please?"

"Jonah, do you remember what I told you the other day?"

"Good behavior, good helper and I get something special?"

"Have you been good?"

"Yes, grandpa. I helped grandma make dinner today."

Jeanie nudged Alvin on the arm.

As I ate and listened to their conversations, I couldn't help but feel a familiarity about the moment. It made me think of Tony and his family who lived across the street. I always thought Tony had the perfect family. I remember dreaming of wanting to be a part of his family.

Alvin took notice of my somber look and asked, "You ok?"

"Yeah, it's nothing."

"Christmas is in a few weeks, Henry. You will enjoy Christmas around here. We have a lot of fun."

I nodded and went back to staring at my plate. The holiday season was always difficult for me. With grandma gone and no immediate family to call on, or a close friend, I dogged holidays with a six-pack of beer and then some.

"Henry, did you like the dinner?"

"Oh yes, it was good. It's been awhile since I've eaten a home cooked meal like this. Thank you."

"You don't cook Henry?"

"Nah, not really. The time I lived with my grandma, I would sit at the table and watch her cook. After she got sick, I took over the cooking. Food didn't taste the same."

"Jeanie loves to cook. I've gained some weight recently because she's been cooking up new recipes."

Jonah interrupted, "Grandpa, can we go see the puppy now?"

"We need to help your grandma clean up."

Jonah picked up his plate and rushed everyone else to clean up too and asked again, "Grandpa, can we go now?"

"Come on Henry, you too. The fresh air will do you some good."

They visited with the neighbor and the puppies next door until Jonah grew tired.

By this time, Jeanie had organized the spare room for Henry.

"Thank you." Henry whispered.

He sat on the bed, closed his eyes, feeling the anxiety setting in. He needed to relax. His body felt like it was caving in from not having a beer. He had become accustomed to drinking every day. That's how he was getting through the loneliness he was carrying around on the inside. He put his hand over his mouth to suppress his cries. It was all too much. Twenty-five-years-old and he had nothing to his name other than grandma's old car. He recalled his grandma's words: "It's not so good to be thinking about having fun all the time. You need to be thinking more about God. Because one day you're going to be an adult and life may get hard and who is going to be there to help you?" Oh, how he needed God's help right now. He lay back in bed, ready to close his eyes, when he heard voices coming from the adjoining wall. They were loud. It was Alvin and Jonah.

"Grandpa, tell me the story."

"What story Jonah?"

"The one with the big fish who eats the man."

"Oh, the Jonah story. I have read that one to you lots of times."

"But I like it."

"Ok, well, I'll read it to you again."

Alvin began, "The man Jonah did not want to obey God. He ran from God and went and hid inside a boat with sailors. That night, a big storm hit the ocean. The sailors looked at Jonah. They blamed him for the storm, so they threw him into the ocean. A giant fish came along and swallowed Jonah."

"Grandpa, the big fish swallowed Jonah?"

"Oh yes, just like that."

"Grandpa, and what did Jonah do?"

"Jonah spent three days inside the fish. Scared of what might happen to him he started to pray."

"Did he pray to God?"

"Yes, he prayed to God, asking him to please forgive him for not obeying him. He begged God to take him out of the fish. Jonah promised he would obey God and be good for the rest of his life."

"What happened to him, grandpa?"

"Well, God forgave him. The fish spit him out into the ocean. Jonah thanked God for saving him. He obeyed by going to the city of Nineveh to tell people about God."

Henry had listened to the entire conversation between Alvin and his grandson. The tears he had been holding back all evening were back again, and this time there was no stopping them. He turned off the lamp. Curled up in bed. Took the pillow and muffled his cries.

CHAPTER THIRTY-FIVE

Sunday, November 21, 1993 (Four days later)

The morning sun filtered through the curtains. Henry buried his face in the pillow, hoping to catch more sleep. Minutes later he was forced to abandon the idea when he heard Alvin's voice through the door.

"Henry, you up?"

Henry had no choice but to get out of bed and open the door.

"We are going to church. Why don't you come with us? We leave in about forty minutes."

Being a small town, there weren't but two churches. We arrived and, once again, I was in a familiar setting. It was as if a bit of my past was stepping into my present. Upon seeing the parking lot, a sudden rush of memories hit me hard. It was the same church grandma attended years back with me in tow. The cross atop the steeple looked weathered, but still in good condition. Overcome with emotion, I quickly wiped my face with the back of my hand. I wasn't about to miss any part of this moment. Additional buildings and a children's play area appeared to be recent additions to the church grounds. My eyes lit up the moment I saw the tall doors. The display of carvings of a man carrying a cross with people around him was as beautiful as ever. Just for old times' sake, I swept my hands over the details. The interior part of the church was pretty much as I remembered it. The green pastel carpet looked a bit worn. Stained glass windows were as pretty as ever. And who couldn't forget those long, hard wooden benches? Grandma always carried a soft cushion with her to sit on the front bench.

I followed Alvin and his family to a bench up front. It was as if just yesterday I was kneeling alongside grandma to pray. She would tell me to pray for my mom. I'd put my little hands together, lower my head and quietly I would talk to a God I couldn't see. Since those days, I have prayed on and off for my mom. Somewhere deep in my heart, I like to think there is still a tender spot for her.

Alvin noticed my wandering look. "Are you okay?"

I cleared my throat. "Yeah, I'm okay."

Soon after the musicians played the walk-in music, a tall, slender man took his place at the pulpit. Issued a brief prayer and opened the book in his hand. He looked at the congregation, paused for a moment, and then returned to his book. It had been years since I had heard anyone speak about God. I had drifted away from church right after grandma's passing. Aside from my brief prayers for my mom, I had little interest in church, sermons, or anything related to religion anymore. This entire church scenario caused me to think about my relationship with a God I couldn't see. Could there be room in my heart for him? And what could this man say today that would help me? Crossed my arms and listened, anyway.

The man began, "We all hear the word of God plain and clear in church, and we all claim to believe in the word of God too; yet it seems the moment we drive out of the parking lot, we forget about it and our disobedience kicks in, just like kids. So it's no surprise to me when I get calls throughout the week, Pastor Bob, I have a problem, Pastor Bob, this happened to me yesterday, Pastor Bob, my husband did this, and on and on and on. And why is it so hard for you all to obey? Could it be your heart is holding on to some form of bitterness, maybe some anger, or maybe it's your unwillingness to forgive that's keeping you from obeying the word of God? Whatever it is, God can help you get back on track to obedience. And when you have obedience in your life, problems you have been living with work themselves out. I'm telling you God is here to give you a better life."

I tried hard to suppress the tears.

The man continued, "Stop barreling around life in a state of confusion. Your life can be so much better. I promise you. You can have an actual home, a better job." He paused for a moment and then started up again, "Take the first steps to a better life today by coming up here to the altar so we can pray for you and your troubles."

Alvin turned to me; "Would you like to go up to the altar?"

I nodded.

"I'll walk with you." Alvin said.

The man at the altar instructed everyone to pray with him, "Father in heaven, forgive me if I have wronged anyone, as I forgive those who have brought wrong into my life, too. I welcome and accept you into my heart today. Amen." The man spoke for a few more minutes longer, then concluded the sermon with, "Those of you who want additional prayer can stay longer. The rest of you, someone at the door, will give each of you some information on how to stay in touch with the church and how to maneuver through your new journey."

Alvin tapped me on the shoulder. "How do you feel?"

"I'm okay."

"I'm so glad you came today. It's all going to get better; you'll see Henry. Let's go find my wife and Jonah. I think they might be over by the door."

Jonah ran up to Alvin the moment he spotted him in the crowd. "Grandpa, look at my paper. I drew a big fish."

Alvin picked up his grandson and gave him a peck on the cheek. "Good coloring. You colored inside the lines very well."

Henry stood by the side and watched as Alvin spilled his affection on his grandson, prompting him to wonder why the boy's mom hadn't been around since his arrival at Alvin's home. Where was she? And where was the boy's father? He wanted to ask, but decided it was none of his business. He just felt happy to be included in their family circle for the time being.

Detecting a sudden change in Henry again, Alvin asked him, "Are you okay? You look like you're lost in your thoughts."

"Nothing important. Hey thanks for bringing me here today. It did my heart good to come here."

CHAPTER THIRTY-SIX

Thursday, December 9, 1993

Henry looked at the calendar. Made a face. Holiday season had arrived and with it, some mixed feelings. He had not celebrated a holiday with anyone in years.

Accustomed to sitting alone in front of the television getting drunk holiday after holiday, this one would finally be different for me because I would get to spend the holiday with Alvin and his family, which meant I would experience the holiday in a whole new light.

Saturday, December 18, 1993 (Days later)

No sooner did Henry sit on the sofa to read the newspaper when he heard Alvin and Jonah having one of their conversations in the kitchen.

"Grandpa, can I write a letter to Santa to tell him to bring Henry's presents here?"

"I think you are sweet to think of, Henry. I tell you what, why don't I help you write the letter tonight?"

"Really grandpa?"

"Yes, but right now you need to finish your breakfast so grandma can take you to get a haircut."

Other than my grandma, I never had a reason to buy presents for others until now. Motivating myself to go out to shop for Alvin and his family could be a challenge with crowds. However, I was determined to get out there and shop. I found the Christmas scene filled with holiday spirit and the crowd of people somewhat chaotic, bringing on a bit of anxiety. I wanted so desperately to feel the joy these people were feeling. It had been so long since I had felt some joy in my heart. Not since my grandma was alive. While walking around, I bought a couple of gifts and then sat on a bench underneath the coolest looking tree. The twisted branches made for a pretty photo meant for a couple walking around, holding hands. I took a deep breath. Stuck my sweaty hands in my pockets and got back on my feet to shop some more.

CHAPTER THIRTY-SEVEN

Saturday, December 25, 1993 (Christmas Day)

Christmas Day arrived and with it an awkward feeling as Henry made his way into the living room. Almost as if he was intruding on a family moment when he saw Alvin and his family, along with a pretty young woman seated around the tree opening presents. Perhaps the young woman was Jonah's mother? Not wanting to interfere in their perfect family moment, he decided he would watch from a distance. It was a glimpse into what real family life looked like in their world.

Upon seeing Henry, Alvin shifted his attention. "Henry, we were wondering how much longer you were going to sleep. You missed breakfast."

"I'm good." Henry replied.

"This is my daughter Becky."

The pretty young woman eyed her father. "Dad, it's Becca. How many times do I have to tell you I changed my name?"

Alvin mumbled, "Becky is a beautiful name."

"It was fitting for a six-year-old back then. I'm a grown woman now!"

Alvin handed Henry some presents. "Henry, these are from us."

Jonah called out, "Open mine first."

Henry reached for Jonah's present and opened it. He smiled. Jonah had added Henry to a family drawing.

Second present was a silver pocket piece engraved with the words, "Guide my way."

Alvin said to him, "You ever get lost in life, pull this out of your pocket. It will guide you."

"Thank you so much."

"Oh, but there is one more for you, Henry. It's from me." Added Jeanie.

Work gloves and they were the perfect size. "Thank you." He said.

Jeanie continued, "Alvin said you lost your work gloves, so I got you another pair. I hope they fit."

"Thank you again. You've given me a nice Christmas to remember."

"Lets go eat." Alvin said as he ushered everyone into the dining room. "Today we are celebrating the gift of a new friendship, but also the gift of family. We are happy to have Becky back home. She's been away from us for over a year."

Becca interrupted, "Dad, you make it sound like I'm back for good. Remember, I'm only here for a few days."

Henry cleared his throat. He wanted to know more about Becky, or was it Becca? Whatever the name, he felt he needed to know more. "Are you in school?" He asked.

Becca laughed, "Hell no. Finished that chapter as soon as I could. I'm a Resource Specialist at one of the Natural State Areas in the state. Live on the grounds year round. Take vacation here and there. Come see mom and dad when I can."

She had the prettiest blue eyes and a spray of freckles on her nose, much like someone else he used to know. He lowered his eyes, pushed his food around the plate. He suddenly felt uncomfortable.

She felt curious to know more about Henry. Her finger swiped a lick off the coconut crème pie on the table. She couldn't handle the mystery anymore. She looked straight across the table at Henry. "So why are you here on Christmas day? Shouldn't you be with your family? Oh wait, don't tell me. You don't have a family. Did my dad pick you up off the side of the road or something? You know he does that a lot."

Alvin interrupted, "Becky, honey, you're being rude. Henry's our guest. He's had a rough time the last few years. We are helping him get back on his feet."

"Really dad? He looks okay to me. You sure you're not trying to replace my brother? Because that's what this looks like to me."

Jeanie held up her hand. Her voice trembling, "Stop it, Becca. You can't just walk in here and bleed your emotions all over someone you don't even know. Your father and I have done the best to help you overcome your hardships over the years. And this is what we get in return? You leave Henry out of this. He is a good man. He just needs some direction. Your focus should be on Jonah. Whether you like it or not, your blood runs through him. At some point, you need to acknowledge him."

Becca took a deep breath. Pushed her chair back. Picked up her plate and said, "Don't tell me I need to acknowledge someone when you two refuse to move on. Dad, it's time for you to let go. You need to acknowledge he's gone." She slammed the patio door as hard as she could.

Jeanie pulled on Alvin's arm, "It's ok. Leave her. She needs time to be alone and to think about her actions. Our meal is getting cold. We better eat."

After Becca's scene, I too stood up. She was right. I had no place in the Beard home and much less on Christmas Day when the family was having a private gathering. Becca's words troubled my mind. Was Alvin really looking to replace the son he'd lost? And why was Jeanie attacking Becca for not being the mother little Jonah deserved? The questions just kept coming at me. Maybe at some point, I could muster enough courage to get some answers. I took a seat in the living room, where it was quiet. Several thoughts later, I concluded the Beard family was no different from any other family. Despite their heavy faith and love for one another, they still experienced the same troubles as me and everyone else.

Some time later, after the family finished eating, they all stepped outside to sit on the back patio, hoping to talk some sense into Becca. As for me, I felt just fine being alone in the living room. I got comfortable. Picked up the photo album on the coffee table. The spirit of love was present in every photo. As I flipped through the photo album, I noticed a familiarity in the photos. Becca's brother looked a lot like Tony. Tony was my childhood friend from across the street. On random weekends, we would play all evening waiting for the moon to show up. We would practice jumping, pretending to reach the moon. I studied the photos again. Could Becca be Tony's little sister, Becky? Never paid much attention to last names when I was young, nor did I ever recall hearing Tony call his parents by their first names. It was always just mom and dad. As I continued flipping through the album, I could feel the anxiety setting in. Take a deep breath. Take a deep breath.

Out of nowhere, I heard a voice.

I turned to see Alvin standing behind the sofa. I closed the album.

Stuck his hands in his pockets and said, "He was a good kid. Had a good heart with a bright future ahead. Didn't deserve to die so young."

I sat still and listened as Alvin came around and sat in a chair across from me.

His voice cracked. "Friday, February 6, 1981. Remember that day as if it were yesterday. Jeanie and I sat up front. Tony was in the back seat. Dressed in his basketball uniform, he kept his attention on his music player. We were on our way to the school for the last game of the season. That day, they had moved the game to seven because the other team experienced some car trouble. We had driven through that intersection, I guess, a million times. That evening, a malfunction of some sorts occurred with the traffic lights. On our side, the traffic lights appeared just fine. The light turned green. I put my signal light on, as I had always come to do. I drove through the intersection to make a left turn. That's when our lives changed forever. The traffic lights on the opposite side of the intersection weren't working. Cars were driving through. The other car must have been driving at a high speed, because the impact crushed the back end of our car. Tony was in the back seat. The firefighters had to cut through the mangled metal to get to Tony. He still had a pulse when they pulled him out. We rushed to the hospital. In a matter of minutes after arriving, our thirteen-year-old son was gone."

Alvin covered his face, trying to keep the emotion from spilling.

I looked away. Take a deep breath. Take a deep breath. How was I supposed to respond to that? Another driver had killed Tony, my childhood friend, in an accident. He didn't get a chance to grow up to experience life. No wonder his sister Becky was on an emotional rollercoaster.

In that moment, I realized the Beard family, as much as myself, were all bleeding the same on the inside. Grief had come and cheated us all of memories we might have made together as friends and as families.

CHAPTER THIRTY-EIGHT

Wednesday, July 13, 1994 (Seven months later)

Finding Alvin at a time in my life when I hit rock bottom was a sure sign God was looking out for me. Not only was Alvin an excellent mentor, but also the father figure I was so desperately missing in my life. He took Jonah and me fishing and taught me to change oil on grandma's old car. I even helped him finish the renovation on the front porch so we could all sit around evening time and watch the cars drive by. When the time came to leave, I gently tucked memories of the past seven months not in my pockets as I had done with my sorrows but in my heart. Being part of a family unit temporarily made all the difference in my life.

"Henry, you sure we can't convince you to stay longer?" Alvin asked.

"No, I've stayed long enough."

Alvin asked, "Well, is there anything we can do to help with getting you started with your new apartment?"

"I'm ok."

"How about furniture?"

Henry responded, "I was thinking maybe I could find some things at a garage sale."

"Hey don't do that! I can call some friends from church to see if they can spare anything."

"You've helped me enough already."

Alvin hugged Henry and said, "We do this because we love you."

CHAPTER THIRTY-NINE

Monday, February 20, 1995
(Several months later)

The experience of living with the Beard family helped me see life in a whole new light. I felt encouraged to think I could one day have a life like Alvin. Perhaps meet the right girl, have a messy house and have kids too. My heart even leaped at the idea of someday seeing my mom again.

However, once the newness and excitement settled down a bit, I felt trapped, lonesome once again. Even my mind felt like it was going in every direction, but in reality, I was going nowhere. I worked as much as I could so I wouldn't have to sit in an empty apartment staring at the walls. Sometimes I made the drive to have dinner with Alvin and his family. Those evenings I felt good. But good didn't hang around for very long. The feeling of restlessness seemed unbearable around evening time. Sometimes the anxiety kicked in so hard I would sweat till my palms were wet. Beer didn't help much other than put me to sleep. The pocket piece Alvin had given me for Christmas didn't do much good either. I decided I would take up running. Someone once told me exercise could help me with my anxiety. They were right. Running through nature trails subdued my anxiety and brought me some much needed peace. I replaced the chaos in my head with the sound of my shoes hitting the ground, but in a good way. Children playing at a distance, people talking to one another along the trails were clear indications the world was on the move. And so was I. Or at least I was trying to move on. Not having any knowledge of my mother's disappearance after so many years still gave me no rest, and no closure in my heart. I needed to talk to Alvin.

CHAPTER FORTY

Tuesday, February 21, 1995 (The following day)

"Henry, how is the apartment?"

"Ok."

"Something wrong?"

Henry cleared his throat, "I'm ok."

"You don't sound ok."

"It's all the idle time I have. I'm not good at it. Start thinking of my grandma. My thoughts then turn to my mom. And I can't go out with the guys from work, because then I get to drinking and I don't know when to stop."

"What happened to getting involved with groups at church?"

"I've never been good at meeting new people."

"The woodworking shop at church needs a couple more guys. I heard they might make toys for kids this year."

Henry covered his eyes and released a choked cry, "I'm sorry, I just don't know..."

"Henry, it's ok, you're not alone. I'm here. I'm going to help you."

Henry took Alvin's advice and joined the woodworking shop at church. It was all he imagined and more. Organized on one wall were many intricate tools. Stacked for easy access on one side of the room were various degrees of wood. And then there was the massive worktable made of the most beautiful birch wood he had ever seen. Henry seemed excited. He fit right in with the group, a bit like fitting into an old comfortable shoe. He soon discovered he could close the door to everyday troubles around him and just focus on making wooden toys. This new chapter in his life brought him much needed peace to his heart. He found a sense of value and worth his life didn't have before.

Six months later.

Henry saved enough money to put a down payment on a home of his own. He was tired of living in an apartment, feeling confined and trapped, as if he were back at the shelter. He wanted a home with more livable space and a small yard. His wish became a reality when Alvin came across an available small house in a neighborhood not too far from his own home. At first sight, Henry felt as if he had traveled back in time. The house had a similar look to the one he lived in with his grandma. There was a sturdy chain-link fence around it. The front door needed some work. A couple of old trees out back shaded the house pretty nicely.

"What do you think?" Asked Alvin.

"I like it. Has everything I need. Except it needs some work."

"You can fix all that. It would also be a wonderful project for you."

"Thank you for all your help. You've been like a father to me."

"I'm here because God knew you were going to need someone to guide you, to help you along the way."

CHAPTER FORTY-ONE

Saturday, April 20, 2002 (Seven years later)

T hanks to Alvin's help over the years, I became more involved in the craftsmanship of
building stuff with my hands. Renovating people's houses along with other side jobs eventually paved the way for me to become a licensed
master carpenter. It became the new chapter
I had hoped to have in my life. Yet somehow,
someway, life always had a way of challenging
me, especially when I felt vulnerable and somewhat weak in spirit.

A trip to the only grocery store in town on
a Sunday afternoon proved to be a bit more
chaotic than I expected. Shoppers pushing
carts through narrow aisles gave way to anxiety.
Ignoring the busy conversations around me, I
quickly grabbed everything I needed and took
my place in line. Picked up a magazine off the
rack when out of the corner of my eye I noticed
her standing behind me. I dared not look at her.
Instead, I put the magazine back, turned my

attention to the candy. I made a face. Not much into sweets. She seemed to be alone.

"Henry, right?" she asked.

I turned around.

It was Becca. Pretty blue eyes with a spray of freckles on her nose. Take a deep breath. Take a deep breath. I pretended not to recognize her.

"I'm sorry, I don't."

"It's me, Becca, don't you remember?"

"Yeah, ok, now I remember." Henry replied.

"So what you shop here too? I thought maybe since you haven't been coming around to see dad, you might be in jail or something."

My palms were getting sweaty. Why was the cashier taking so long? Was there a problem? Maybe if I went to another line, it would move much faster and I could disengage myself from Becca's humiliation.

"Actually, I'm staying pretty busy."

"Oh yeah? Doing what?"

"I bought a house in the area. I'm renovating it."

She curled her smile. "Huh! You should celebrate. Come have a drink with me. I'm on my way to a place down the street. I came in to get some cigarettes."

"Nah, I'm ok. I'm in the middle of finishing a wall."

"Hey, your wall can wait."

"I don't drink anymore."

"Oh, that's stupid!"

It was finally my turn to check out. I quickly picked up my bag and walked away. I could hear Becca's voice behind me. "Henry, one drink won't hurt you. Think about it."

An hour later.

He had lied about finishing a wall. The wall and everything else were done. He inspected every room in the house to see if he needed to do any touch-ups. Nope. It all looked good. The idea of having a drink with Becca sure seemed inviting. Besides, one drink couldn't possibly do any harm. He could go for about an hour, have that one drink, and then come home. Sounded easy enough.

On his way out the door, he picked up his cap and set of keys.

He arrived feeling anxious. Nothing had changed since his last visit. Cigarette smoke was everywhere. The same group of people still hung around complaining and feeling sorry for their troubled lives. He approached the bar. The shiny liquor display had so many choices, and the beer tab over to the left looked even more inviting. A nice cold beer would be perfect. He could drink it nice and slow. It would also give him a chance to relax while he waited for Becca.

The bartender served him a nice cold beer.

Henry took a deep breath and held on to the glass of beer, contemplating to drink it or not. Shook his head. Rubbed his neck. Pushed the beer away. It was a mistake to come here. He had overcome his heavy drinking years back. Why mess his life up again? Decided it was best to leave. As he made his way towards the door, he saw her sitting in a corner by herself. She had gone home and changed. She was wearing a pretty floral dress with those crazy wedge heels all the girls were currently wearing. A light floral scent lingered around her. She smiled. It meant something. He approached her table.

"You came." She said.

Feeling the anxiety setting in again, Henry shoved his hands in his pockets. Should have drank the beer. How could she be so pretty and yet have such a foul mouth?

Her eyes lit up. "Sit down, Henry. I'm not going to bite you."

He couldn't resist. Take a deep breath. He pulled a chair. Take a deep breath.

Becca smiled. "Relax Henry, we're just having a drink. It's not like we're going to have sex."

He was going to need more than a beer to get through five minutes of conversation, so he ordered a specialty drink, hoping it would help him relax.

The five-minute conversation turned into all evening event of drinking, laughing and even dancing. Just two childhood friends getting acquainted all over again.

He whispered, "I've always liked you, Becky." He looked into her pretty blue eyes. "Since we were kids."

She whispered back, "Me too."

They continued dancing.

CHAPTER FORTY-TWO

Sunday, April 21, 2002 (The following day)

A dog barking outside Henry's window was making it difficult to enjoy the last moments of his sweet dream. He squeezed his pillow, then turned to his side, hoping he could keep the dream alive for a bit longer. Not a chance. Opened his eyes, looked around the room. Had last night really happened? Or was it all a dream? His head was throbbing. Reached for the aspirin on the nightstand. Decided a shower might do him some good. An hour later, he took to the sofa to think about last night's outing. Before long, he'd fallen into a deep sleep.

Several hours later, a knock on the door interrupted his deep sleep. He rolled over. He wanted to enjoy the moment on the sofa longer. Maybe that someone at the door would tire of knocking and go away. Nope. The knocking continued. Take a deep breath.

He opened the door to see a woman and a young girl standing on his doorstep.

Henry gave them a puzzling look.

"Are you Henry Odin?" Lady asked.

"What do you want?"

"Can we come in?"

He felt his headache returning.

"Please, can we come in?" Lady persisted.

"I don't know you. Why would I let you come inside my house?"

"I've come to drop off your daughter."

Henry's tired expression turned into fear. "Daughter?" He asked.

"Yes, your daughter."

His temples were now throbbing. "You've made a mistake. I'm not; I don't even have a girlfriend." He attempted to close the door.

In defiance, the woman held up her hand. "Look, it's raining. Can we come in and I'll explain?"

He tightened his grip on the door. "Explain what?"

"Sara Montes, her name was Sara Montes."

"I don't know who you're talking about. You have the wrong house." He started to close the door again.

"Wait, I have proof. She is your daughter."

Henry eyed the woman and then the young girl. "Proof?"

"Yes." The woman replied.

Wow! What dream had he stepped into?

Henry kept a steady eye on them. They

sat on the sofa while he kept his distance in a chair across from them. After last night's outing with Becca; he felt vulnerable and uneasy. Didn't want to be taken advantage of. He cast his eyes at the young girl. At thirteen-years-old she had a petite frame and was on the skinny side. She wore a pair of shorts, a T-shirt and sneakers with her hair pulled back. Her eyes were a pretty green. He recalled his mother having green eyes, too. He needed to pull himself together.

"So where's the proof?" He asked.

The woman handed him a large envelope. After scanning through the documents, he handed them back to her and said. "You think you can come in here with fake papers and I'm just going to believe she's my daughter? Who sent you? Is this like a prank or something?" He rubbed his forehead. A sign he was feeling tired and needed to get back to bed.

The woman turned to the young girl, "Jenny, show him your birth mark. It will proof you're his daughter."

Henry looked stunned. The young girl had a birthmark just like the one under his left arm. Hers, however, was smaller.

The woman pointed to the young girl. "You think this is a coincidence?"

Silence hung in the air.

Henry eyed the young girl again, "Ok well,

what if she is my daughter? Are you looking for money?"

"It's not like that at all."

"Where is her mother? Why didn't she come?"

The woman's voice choked up. "I have my two children to take care of. Last week I lost my job, so now I can't take care of Jenny anymore. She gets a hundred dollars a month from a special fund her mother left her. It's not enough to feed, clothe and take care of all her needs."

The agitation set in. "Where is her mother?" Henry asked again.

"Sara died in a car accident six months ago."

"I'm sorry. How did it happen?"

The lady could barely keep her composure. "It was at night. There was a thunderstorm. She lost control on the highway and hit another car. If I had not stepped up to take Jenny in, at this moment she might be living at a shelter for teenagers."

Henry turned to the young girl. "I'm sorry about your mother."

The woman added, "She used to talk about you all the time after she met you. She thought you and her were going to have something together. And when it didn't work out, she was upset. Months later, she found out she was pregnant. It was like the greatest gift she had ever received. Jenny became her life."

Henry handed her the box of tissues.

The woman wiped her teary face and said. "She was an amazing mother to Jenny."

"Why didn't Sara look for me?"

"Sara was afraid if she went looking for you and told you about the baby; you might try to take the baby from her. She decided she would raise the baby by herself."

Jenny held on to the woman's hand.

Henry shook his head, "I can't. I can't care for anyone right now."

The woman begged Henry; "I have all her belongings in my car. Please. She is a good girl. She can help with the cleaning and the cooking."

Closed his eyes for a moment. Was he being punished for having drinks last night with Becca, or what? He looked at the young girl again and asked her, "Your birth certificate reads Jennifer. Do you like being called Jennifer or Jenny?"

"Jenny."

Shook his head in disbelief. His anxiety was setting in. Take a deep breath. Take a deep breath.

Looked at Jenny once again, then at the woman, "I'm sorry, it's too much responsibility for me."

The woman's tone changed from pleasant to anger and then to crying. "How can you say no to taking your own daughter? Look at her, your blood runs through her veins. She even looks like you."

Henry stood up, walked over to the window. No doubt in his mind he was being punished for last night's event. Darkness was trying to seep back into his life. Rubbed the stubble on his chin back and forth, trying to keep his anxiety from getting out of control. Take a deep breath. Take a deep breath. He knew nothing about fatherhood. He questioned himself on the inside if he could even care for another person. But then how was he going to let her go to some kind of shelter, knowing the possibility existed she could very well be his daughter? He turned around to face them once again.

"Okay, she can stay."

The woman whispered, "Thank you." She nudged Jenny. "Lets go get your things from the car."

Henry followed behind to help unload.

After everything was unloaded, the woman hugged Jenny and gave Henry a piece of paper. "Here is my number. Jenny can call me anytime."

Jenny begged the woman, "Please, I don't want to stay here. I'm afraid."

The woman hugged Jenny again. "You're going to be fine. This man is your father. He is going to take good care of you." She wiped Jenny's tears. "You call me anytime you want."

After the woman drove off, Jenny followed Henry back inside the house.

"Where am I going to sleep?" Jenny asked.

Take a deep breath. Take a deep breath. "There are two empty bedrooms down the hallway. You can look and see which one you like." Henry replied.

Jenny walked through the rooms in silence. One room was too small. The other room had two windows, a bed, and an old dresser.

"I know the room is small and there's not much stuff in here, but if you like, I can buy you some other things." Henry said.

She turned to look at Henry.

To calm the fear in her eyes, he said, "I'm not going to hurt you. I'm not that kind of person."

She said nothing.

He added, "Why don't you rest? We can talk later."

Closed the door and just as he was about to walk away, he heard Jenny's muffled cries. If only he could go back into the room and talk to her, but then feared the conversation between the two might not go well, so he turned away instead. It was time for him to get some rest, too. Last night's outing was still on his mind. At some point, he would need to talk with Becca to find out how she was feeling about last night's event. He made his way to the sofa. Reached for a pillow and got comfortable. Closed his eyes.

Several hours later, when he opened his eyes, he found himself in complete darkness. Sat up, rubbed his face, trying to wake up from a heavy sleep, hoping the day's past events had all been one big dream. As his mind drifted back to the present, he realized it had all happened in real time. He had become a father in a blink of an eye. How would he handle this new chapter in his life? What could he say to Jenny to make her feel better? Other than the short time he had spent with his grandma; he had no basis, no foundation from his childhood to help him here. The palms of his hands were feeling clammy. Maybe if he bought himself a six-pack of beer, it would help him calm down. After a minute, he shoved the thought aside. The responsibility of taking care of a kid or rather a teenager was now a big priority in his life.

Minutes later, it was time to face the inevitable.

He knocked on the bedroom door.

Silence.

He knocked again.

Silence.

"Jenny." He called out.

Silence.

"Jenny, can I come in?"

He heard a slight whisper on the other side of the door.

She was sitting on the edge of the bed, watching the raindrops hit the window when he opened the door. Henry put his hands in his pockets. This scene reminded him of a time when he was eight-years-old and he too was being shuffled around with his belongings. Remembering suffering in silence, refusing to speak to anyone, he knew all too well what she was feeling.

"It's all going to get better, you'll see." He said.

She whispered again, "How? How is it going to get better? I lost my mom, my friends, and I'm in this weird house with a stranger. How is it going to get better?" Her eyes welled up with tears.

Henry swallowed hard. "I know how you're feeling. I was in a similar situation when I was very young. One day, my mother left our apartment and never returned. Days later, I went to live with a grandma I had never met before. I, too, felt scared. In the end, it all turned out ok. In fact, those years with my grandma turned out to be the best of my life."

Silence.

"Tomorrow I will take you to school to sign you up for classes."

Silence.

"Right now, I need to make something to eat. I haven't eaten nothing today. Could be why I don't feel so good right now. Would you like something to eat?"

Silence.

"I'll put a plate in the fridge for you. You can eat whenever you're ready."

As Henry left the room, Jenny approached the window. Rain in the darkness had a rather unsettling look and feel about it, coloring her mood into an even deeper medium of sadness. Just yesterday, her life looked promising with people who adored and cared for her since infancy. Friends of the last seven years were gone. Soon, her past would all be a blur. She could feel the fear settling in around her. Her eyes welled up with tears again. What would become of her life? The idea of living with a strange man scared her. Tomorrow she would go to a new school. What would the kids be like? Would they like her? It was all too much to think about. She threw herself on the bed again and cried into the pillow until she fell asleep.

It was well past midnight when she woke up. She sat up in bed in the dark and hugged her stomach. The hunger pains were unbearable.

She tiptoed through the living room to get to the kitchen. Henry was fast asleep on the sofa. Wrappers of some sort littered the coffee table. The television displayed a picture of fuzzy snow.

"What are you looking for?"

Jenny jerked her head around to see Henry waking up.

"I'm thirsty."

"I'm sorry, didn't mean to scare you. Let me get you some water. Would you like to eat too?"

"Yes."

"Sit down. I'll warm up the plate for you."

Henry pulled out a chair and sat down, too. He wasn't much into conversation, so he sat quietly while she ate.

She ate as fast as she could, and then politely excused herself. "Thank you for the food. I want to go back to the room." She said.

"Yes, it's been a long day, and tomorrow will be a busy day, too." He said.

He sat back in the chair, titled his head back. What had he gotten himself into? He needed some kind of drink to help him relax. His anxiety was making his palms sweaty. Opened the refrigerator to see milk and orange juice as his two choices of drink. He chose the latter. Sat on the sofa again. His thoughts drifted back to his childhood days, thinking of his mother. His heart still longed for her return. If only to know what happened the night she disappeared. His thoughts came back to the present, thinking of

the situation with Jenny and how she was missing her mother, too. He feared not being able to
parent the girl. He drank the last of the juice.
Turned off the lights and went to bed.

CHAPTER FORTY-THREE

Monday, April 22, 2002 (The following day)

Jenny wandered into the kitchen wearing a short plaid skirt, white shirt, and ballet flats.

Henry shook his head in disbelief. "Go change into something else, please!" He said.

"Why?"

"Because I think the skirt is too short."

"Everyone wears these skirts."

"Well, you're not everyone. You're living here in my house and I don't need you getting pregnant the first week of school, so go change."

She slammed the bedroom door behind her.

He called out, "And breakfast is ready."

Minutes later, Jenny was back in the kitchen. She had changed into jeans, a T-shirt, and sneakers.

Henry took a deep breath. "Much better." He said.

She sat down, pursed her lips, when she saw eggs, beans rolled up in a tortilla on a plate. "What's this?" She said.

"Breakfast. My grandma used to make it for

breakfast when I was young. Though I could never eat the taco like that, I always had to have the eggs, beans and the tortilla separated."

She stood up. "I'm not hungry. Can we go now?"

"Well, give me a minute. I'm finishing up the lace on my boot." He looked up at her. "I don't see a backpack."

"Do I need one?" She responded.

"Do you even have one?"

"Yeah."

"Well, go get it."

We made the drive to school in silence except for the nervous tick Jenny was having with her pencil, tapping it on the seat and twirling it back and forth. She kept her teary eyes to the side window.

I knew all too well what she was thinking and the fear she was feeling. If only I could tell her all would be ok, though in my mind I knew it would not make a bit of difference to her.

The car came to a stop in front of a small building.

"This is the school?" She asked.

"Yes, what's wrong?"

"It's old and where's the rest of the buildings? How are all the kids supposed to fit in there?"

"We live in a small town. The population here is smaller. The schools here don't need to be as big as the ones in the city."

"I want to go to another school. A school that's new."

"Jenny, you'll be fine. In a week, you'll make some new friends and you won't care so much about the building."

Registration for classes took but fifteen minutes. Afterwards, Henry gave Jenny some money for lunch. She grabbed the money out of his hand, turned her back, and walked away.

"I'll be outside waiting when the school bell rings this afternoon." He said to her.

She kept walking.

By the end of the day, Jenny was ready to be done with school. She looked at the clock on the classroom wall. Relieved to see the hour. Soon she would go home. Run into her room so she could be alone to cry. When the bell rang, she walked outside as fast as she could. Henry was already waiting. She got into the car and slammed the door.

"How was your day? Make any friends?" He asked.

"I don't want to talk about it."

Noting her mood, he started the car and drove off. Once on the highway, Jenny noticed the commute differed somewhat from the morning commute.

"Why is it taking so long to get to the house?" She asked.

Henry responded, "We are going to see a doctor, take some blood tests. I want to be certain you and I are father and daughter. I don't want to be living with doubts."

To avoid any further humiliation from Henry, Jenny kept her mouth shut, turned to the side window and kept her eyes steady on the winding roads.

They arrived at the clinic in silence. Within the hour, they were back on the road headed home.

Jenny was the first one to get out of the car, slamming the door behind her.

She rushed into the house. Ran to her room. Threw herself on the bed and cried into her pillow. "Hate this place! I want my mom and my friends back."

Henry trailed behind her. "I'm sorry you are in this situation. Give it some time. You'll make some friends."

She cried out, "Go away. Leave me alone."

He closed the door behind him. It was apparent Jenny's emotions were all over the place. It was enough to drive anyone over the edge. Fortunately for him, Alvin had come along when God knew he needed help. Now it was going to be his turn to help Jenny.

He cleaned up and went straight to the refrigerator; he needed to drink something cold and soothing before getting to dinner.

Perhaps a beer might help him with the anxiety he was experiencing. Parenting a thirteen-year-old daughter would not be easy. She had quite a personality in her. He took a sip of cold water before deciding it would be best if he sat on the sofa to think about the situation at hand.

"What happens if I'm not your daughter?" She asked.

Henry jerked his head around to see Jenny standing behind the sofa. Her face was a mess. She hadn't stopped crying since they arrived home.

"Come sit down." He motioned.

"What's going to happen to me?"

He studied her for a moment. She had inherited quite a few of his qualities. Her dark hair was definitely from his side, something his mother always hated about him and would probably hate about her, too. He recalled how she thought dark hair made him look ugly and yet on Jenny; it was beautiful. And then there was the mole under the arm, her nose and her height. How could she not be his daughter? Still, he had to be certain.

"We'll get the test results in a few weeks. For now, let's not worry about it." He took another sip of cold water. Fixed his composure, and headed back into the kitchen.

"But."

"No but. Let's work on getting dinner. I'm hungry, and I'm sure you're hungry, too."

She wiped her teary eyes and followed him into the kitchen.

"What are we going to eat?" She asked.

"I was thinking maybe a turkey sandwich. My grandma used to make sandwiches all the time. She could cook anything in minutes and it would always taste delicious."

Jenny eased up a bit and pulled a chair to sit.

"Were you sad when your mom disappeared?" She asked.

"Yes, I was. There were a lot of tears back in those days. Never saw her again after that night. Thing is I always have her on my mind. Even after all these years, I still have the hope that one day I will see her again. She wasn't the best mother, but my heart still loves her."

"What about your grandma?"

"The police connected her with me. She was generous enough to take me in. She passed away before I went off to college. Over the years, I've had a friend who has always been there to help me. You will get to meet him and his family soon. Okay, let's eat."

He watched Jenny devour her sandwich. The scene reminded him of when he too was young, always hungry, devouring whatever food someone would place in front of him.

"Can I have more?"

"You can have as many as you want." He fixed her another sandwich; joined her at the table again. For the first time in a long time, he had someone to share the dinner table with. It felt good. Maybe good could hang around longer this time.

"How did you like your classes today?"

"The PE class is too much work."

"You don't like to play sports?"

"I don't like to sweat."

He laughed.

"Do you have homework?"

"Yeah."

"You have all evening to get it done."

When they finished dinner, Jenny helped Henry clean the kitchen.

"I see you clean up and wash pretty good. From now on, this might end up being your chore around here."

When all the cleaning was done, Henry opened the refrigerator. He poured more cold water into his glass.

"Do you drink a lot of cold water?"

Henry stared at the glass in his hand. She had no idea what he was going through at the moment.

"It's like your second glass of water."

He smiled. "Are you counting?"

"No, I don't like to count, calculate numbers, or do anything with math."

Henry could feel the anxiety dissipating as he laughed.

"Why are you laughing?"

"You and I have another thing in common."

"What?"

"Math. I used to have problems with math all the time when I was younger."

They continued the conversation in the living room.

After a while, Henry shifted his conversation. "I think I've talked enough about me. Why don't you tell me something about yourself?"

Jenny shrugged her shoulders. "Like what?"

"Tell me what you like to do. What do you like to eat? Do you have any goals or dreams of what you want to do when you finish school?"

Jenny started feeling uneasy. Even though the man sitting next to her was supposed to be her father, she had only met him a day before. He was very much a stranger in her eyes.

"My friends and I used to have sleepovers every Friday. We would eat pizza and listen to music."

Henry couldn't help but notice how well she articulated herself. It was obvious her mother had cared for and loved her very much. And now it was his turn to continue molding and shaping her life so she could go out into the world prepared for anything.

"Anything else?" He asked.

"I, well, my mom was sending me to piano lessons before she had the accident."

"Did you learn to play some music?"

Jenny became quiet and lowered her head.

"It's okay if you can't talk about it."

She took a deep breath and continued, "I learned how to play a little. I would play for my mom." She hesitated, and then continued again. "Mom used to say music softens the heart when we are angry or hurting."

"Looks like you had a great mom. I'm so sorry that I don't remember much about her. It's been many years. Tell me something else about your mom."

"Mom used to love to go shopping, especially for shoes. She had all these shoes." Jenny covered her face. "I can't."

"It's okay, you don't have to continue. I understand your heart is still very tender. I get that. It's going to take time before your heart can feel strong again."

Jenny wiped her teary eyes and ran back into her room.

Henry reclined back on the sofa, looked around the room. He rubbed his sweaty palms. He felt overwhelmed. But what was making him feel that way? The drinking had stopped some time back, so he couldn't put the blame on that. It was his own ignorance he felt concerned with. He lacked all the required qualities to be a parent. Having been a teenager himself once, he still didn't understand all the things involved with teenagers. Especially with teenage girls. He needed to talk to someone; otherwise he felt he would end up losing more than just himself. Minutes later, he cleared the coffee table and went to his room. He was tired. An early night to bed would help clear up his mind. Maybe tomorrow he could think with clarity and find direction.

CHAPTER FORTY-FOUR

Tuesday, May 14, 2002

Henry glanced at the calendar. It had been a few weeks since he and Jenny had taken blood tests. Thinking about the situation and the outcome made him feel anxious.

Despite all the similarities between him and Jenny, he was finding it hard to believe she was his daughter. And today would prove even more difficult if the blood tests returned with positive results. It would mean he would have to man up and learn to take care of someone other than himself. Could he do it?

He walked over to the refrigerator. Slammed it back shut. He was tired of drinking cold water. What he needed was a beer. It would help him drown out all the emotional chaos he was feeling on the inside. His palms were sweating again. Take a deep breath. Take a deep breath. It was time to pick up the test results. On his way out the door, he grabbed his baseball cap and keys.

"Mr. Odin, here are your results. Can you please sign the last two pages?"

He could feel a slight chill seep through him as he took the large envelope.

"If you should have questions, please call us."

He nodded.

The drive home felt like hours away, yet it was only twenty minutes. He couldn't wait to get home to open the envelope. The moment he arrived, he hurried inside, only to come to a stop when he placed the envelope on the coffee table. Take a deep breath. Take a deep breath. He needed to sit and think about how he was going to approach the results. He tilted his head backwards and closed his eyes. Moments later, he regained his composure. The clock on the wall showed he had plenty of time to go buy a beer and study the results. He shook his head. He was an idiot. How was beer going to help in this situation? In fact, it could very well hinder the father and daughter relationship he was try-ing to build with Jenny. A part of him was ex-cited, hoping Jenny was indeed his daughter. He picked up the envelope. Fear settled in right next to him. What if she wasn't his daughter? How would he tell her? Would he continue rais-ing her? His mind was spiraling, and not in a good way. Several minutes later, he glanced at the clock again. Soon, he would have to go get Jenny from school. He felt his anxiety setting in. His palms were sweaty again. The envelope would have to wait for another time. He splashed cold water on his face; changed shirts and headed out the door.

Jenny stood by the front of the school, sheltering from the sun. Looking for Henry until she found his car in the parking lot. The moment Henry spotted her, he felt an unexpected rush of emotion. He couldn't imagine sending her away, even if she wasn't his daughter. She had no one else who could care for her. He wasn't about to let her go spend the rest of her teen years in some shelter. Not that it was a terrible place or anything, but it didn't provide the love, the warmth and security of a family.

"How was your day?" Henry asked.

"Boring."

Henry laughed, "Why do you say that?"

"We had to take practice tests on stuff I already know."

"That's good. It means you're ahead of your class."

"I guess."

"You hungry?"

"Yes. Can we eat pizza today? I'm tired of those beans you cook."

Henry laughed again, "No, those beans I make are nutritious. They are good for you."

Jenny gave him a side eye glance.

Henry smiled, "Ok, pizza it is."

The Italian eatery in town was a few blocks away from home. They walked into an aroma of sweet Italian herbs. The red and white picnic linens throughout the dining area displayed a family friendly establishment. Wall size murals of Italian cities were on full display. A server escorted Henry and Jenny to a corner table.

"You know what you want?" Henry asked Jenny.

She nodded.

The server made his way back to the table with a delicious dish of fresh baked bread and a dish of homemade butter.

Henry was the first to speak. "My daughter would like a lemonade and for me a beer."

Jenny stared at Henry, somewhat bewildered.

The server gathered the menus; "Are you ready to order too?"

"Yes, we want a large pepperoni pizza with light sauce."

When the server walked away, Jenny couldn't contain her excitement. "Did you say, daughter?"

"It's ok if you don't want to call me dad. Henry is good."

"Did you get the results back? So I'm your daughter?"

He could see the tears blurring her beautiful green eyes.

She reached over and hugged him. "Thank you."

"Careful, don't make me cry, because then I can't stop." Tears were blurring his eyes too.

"You're crying?" Jenny asked.

"Yes, I get emotional knowing I have a daughter and I am no longer alone. I feel like I now have a purpose in life."

"What's that?"

"To be a good parent."

Jenny lowered her eyes.

"What's wrong?" Henry asked.

"You're drinking a beer. People drink and I get scared."

"Thought I could celebrate with one beer. It's been a while since I've had one. I'll drink water then. So why do you get scared when people drink?"

"My mom's dad would drink all the time. He would say awful things to her and to me."

"Sometimes alcohol can do that to people if they can't control it. I had a hard time with it too for a while. But now I'm ok."

CHAPTER FORTY-FIVE

Feeling content in his heart, Henry hummed one of his favorite tunes as he made the drive home with Jenny.

"What is that?" Jenny asked.

"You mean my humming?"

"It sounds like my piano music."

"You'll get to hear it when I take you to church this Sunday."

Jenny's tone changed. "Church? It's been weeks since I got here. You never talk about church."

"Because I wanted to be sure you were..." Henry's voice trailed off.

Jenny felt a slight chill come over her. "Go ahead say it. You don't want to tell them you have a daughter."

"Yes, I kept you a secret from my friends. I wasn't ready to tell them about you until I was sure you were going to be staying."

"Do you not want me to stay here?"

"No Jenny, it's nothing like that. I didn't want to get us all situated as father and daughter, and then something happens."

Jenny could feel a sting in her eyes.

"As excited as I am to have a daughter, I don't have a basis or a real foundation on how to raise a kid, much less a teenage daughter. Truth is, I'm scared."

Jenny wiped her teary eyes and kept quiet for the rest of the drive home.

When they arrived home, Jenny ran inside to clean up her face so Henry couldn't see her dried up tears. Soon after, she joined Henry in the living room.

"What are you doing?" Jenny asked.

"It's something my grandma started when I was a kid. Lighting a candle and praying for my mom helps me to believe she's still out there somewhere." Henry sighed. "I'm sorry I get wrapped up in my past sometimes. Were you going to say something?"

"Do I have to go to church tomorrow?"

"Well, yes, because it's part of my life. I want you to experience it too. Besides, we could both use some help right now." He removed his cap. "My friend Alvin and his family came along and rescued me out of one of my darkest moments in life. I'm grateful for his help. And speaking of Alvin, I need to call him."

Henry picked up the phone and dialed.

"Alvin." He said.

"Henry, we haven't seen you in a few weeks.

Everyone is asking about you. Is everything ok with you?"

"I've been having a bit of a problem with something. It's finally fixed. We will be there on Sunday."

"Ok, we'll see you there."

The weird look on Alvin's face prompted Jeanie to ask, "Who were you talking to?"

"It was Henry. Something about a problem. He says it's fixed and he'll see us at church on Sunday."

"Why do you have that weird look on your face, then?"

"Well, before he hung up, he said, we will be at church."

Jeanie broke out in a smile. "Henry must have a girlfriend."

Alvin scratched his head. "I don't know. He didn't say."

"Well then, we will have to wait and see on Sunday."

"Yes we will."

CHAPTER FORTY-SIX

Sunday, May 19, 2002 (Days later)

Sunday morning couldn't have arrived fast enough. Alvin, Jeanie, and Becca seated themselves so they could wait for Henry to walk through the church doors.

Jeanie nudged Alvin the moment she saw Henry appear, "Look, Henry walked in with a girl." She said.

"What girl?" Becca asked.

Alvin watched as they made their way towards them. "I don't know, but she looks young."

Becca drew her eyebrows in. "Oh my goodness, she's a kid."

Alvin rubbed his forehead. "We need to talk to Henry."

"Yes, before he gets himself into problems." Jeanie said.

Alvin scratched his head and said, "On the phone the other day, he said he fixed the problem."

Jeanie looked at Becca and said, "Oh no, you think?"

Becca responded, "I don't know what to think right now, but look, here he comes."

Henry approached the bench. "Hey friends, this is Jenny."

Alvin and Jeanie greeted them in a somewhat crusty manner while Becca ignored them altogether.

Henry continued the introductions, "This is Alvin and his wife, Jeanie, over there is Becca, their daughter."

Alvin took a deep breath, looked at Henry, then at Jenny. A silence circulated around them until Jeanie motioned to sit down.

During the service, Becca couldn't help but notice Henry's affection for Jenny. He laughed and whispered in her ear a few times. He even put his arm around her.

When the service was over, Becca dismissed herself to go get Jonah from bible class, so that Alvin could invite Henry and Jenny to have lunch at a restaurant around the corner. He needed to know more about the Henry and Jenny situation.

Both families arrived at the restaurant crowded with its usual regulars all occupying the round tables in each corner. Others appeared to be engaged in some much needed laughter. Instead of ordering from the menu, the Beard family all ate from the buffet. It seemed the easiest way to keep occupied without having to ask Henry about Jenny.

Minutes passed, and neither party spoke to one another. Focused on their food until Henry asked, "Can someone please pass the salt?"

Alvin and Jeanie dropped their forks.

Henry looked at them. "What's wrong?"

Becca was the first one to speak. "Nothings wrong with us." She pointed her fork at Henry and said, "But it looks like there's something definitely wrong with you."

Henry made a face. "What?"

Everyone looked at each other in confusion.

Alvin sighed before speaking, "Henry, the girl. Don't you think she is much too young for you?"

Henry laughed, "I'm sorry, I didn't tell you?"

Becca made a face. "Tell us what?"

"Jenny is my daughter."

Alvin interrupted, "Your daughter?"

"Years ago, I had a thing with a girl. She never reached out to me when she discovered she was pregnant. I knew nothing about Jenny's existence until a few weeks ago, when she showed up at my doorstep with one of her mother's friends."

Alvin and Jeanie looked at Jenny. "Where's your mom?"

Jenny responded, "She died in a car accident."

Jeanie stood up and hugged her. "We are so sorry."

Alvin chimed in, "But we are happy you found your father."

Henry asked, "So why were you all acting so weird?"

Alvin laughed, "Oh, we thought you, her, you know."

Henry broke out laughing, too. "You thought she was my girlfriend?"

Jeanie laughed, "Yes."

"No, Jenny is way too young for a man like me."

Alvin interrupted, "Jeanie and I were thinking the same thing."

Becca added, "And I was getting ready to poke you with the fork."

Henry continued laughing.

"Oh yes, mom and dad were so upset with you." Becca said.

Henry couldn't contain his laughter. "I should have said something sooner."

Alvin hugged Henry. "This is the best thing that's happened to you. A daughter! Wow! So have you decided if you want Jenny to call you dad or just Henry?"

"This is all so sudden. I don't know, think it's up to Jenny."

Jenny wrinkled her nose and smiled.

CHAPTER FORTY-SEVEN

Saturday, May 25, 2002

Jenny walked into the kitchen to find Henry sitting at the table, having his third cup of coffee. She asked him, "Have you seen my sneakers?"

"No."

"I thought I left them by the front door."

"Jenny, why are you fidgeting with your hands? Something wrong?"

She came back into the kitchen. Took a deep breath and said, "I'm excited you're my father, but I'm not ready to call you dad." She wrinkled her nose. "It's kind of weird."

"It's ok Jenny, this is all new to both of us."

She took a deep breath again. "Is it ok if I still call you Henry?"

"Of course." He pulled out a chair. "Sit down a moment."

He took his cap off, combed his hair back and began, "Even though it's been over a month since you moved in, I think it's going to take some time for you and I to adjust to one another. I think more for me than you."

"Why?"

"Well, for starters, I've lived alone for a long time. On and off, I've battled a problem with alcohol. There are anxiety issues I'm still working through. You need a father who can care for you and be around when you need him."

"I think you're ok."

"Ok, is not enough. You need a father who is encouraging, who can help you navigate life the right way. Not some loser who is always thinking about how quickly he can get his hands on a beer so he can blur out everything and everyone around him."

She whispered, "I can help you."

"Thank you. This is a battle I have to fight on my own, up here, in my mind. It's the only way to fix my problem."

A sudden knock on the front door interrupted the conversation.

Jenny's eyes lit up. "My friend is here." She said.

Henry stood up, put his cap back on, and said. "I'm going to do some work on the porch."

While Jenny ushered her friend inside, Henry was ready to greet the warm weather outside. He gathered his tools. His plan was to work on the porch railing. An hour later, his project came to a halt when he heard a loud cry coming from the back of the house. He dropped everything and rushed inside.

Jenny's friend came running through the back door.

"Mr. Odin, it's Jenny. She hurt her foot. She's bleeding all over the patio."

Fear seeped in. Take a deep breath. Take a deep breath. He felt he couldn't move fast enough to get to the first aid kit. Where was it? He searched the bathroom and every cabinet in the kitchen till he found it. When he stepped out the back door, he found Jenny sitting on the ground, holding onto her foot, crying in pain.

"Dad, hurry, it hurts."

"Yes, Jenny, hold on. I need to check to see where all the blood is coming from. Might be from your big toe. Don't move. I need to clean it."

"Ouch, it stings." Jenny cried.

"Yes, I know, hold on. I'm wrapping it up. Can you walk?"

"No."

"Not even a little?"

"Dad, don't be funny. It hurts a lot."

"Ok then, I'll carry you to the car."

"Where are we going?"

"I'm taking you to the emergency room at the hospital. Have to get your toe checked. Don't want you to lose your toe."

They arrived to find the waiting room overflowing into the lobby. Henry and Jenny had no choice but to wait. Blood seeping through the bandages prompted a doctor to see Jenny sooner than later.

In examining Jenny's foot, the doctor asked, "How did you hurt your foot?"

Jenny clenched her teeth for a moment and then spoke, "I was kicking the ball with my friend. My foot slipped and landed on a sharp metal thing on the grass."

The doctor looked at Henry. "What kind of sharp metal thing?"

"Some metal border used to mark my property and the neighbors. It's rusty and old."

"You should replace it with something else." The doctor shifted his attention back to Jenny. "And you, young lady, you should not be playing outside barefoot. Good thing there's no damage to the nerves. A few stitches and you'll be on your way."

A short time later, they were back on the road going home when Henry gave Jenny a side eye glance and said, "You called me dad."

"I was in a lot of pain. It slipped out."

"No, it's ok. I liked it. It made me feel needed. Something I haven't felt in a long time. Thank you."

When they arrived home, Jenny went straight to her room to lie down while Henry took to the sofa. He didn't feel motivated to work on the porch railing anymore. He picked up the newspaper instead.

An hour later, Jenny was back. "Dad, my foot is hurting."

Henry looked at his daughter. She used the word dad again. It felt humbling to know she welcomed him as her father.

"It must be time for medicine. Let me get it." He said.

Chapter Forty-Eight

Monday, May 27, 2002

Henry was in the middle of tying laces on his work boots when he noticed Jenny making her way to the kitchen.

"You feeling better?" He asked.

"Sort of."

"How is your foot?"

"It hurts a little."

"I see you're dressed. I guess you want to go to school?"

"I'll walk slow."

"I was hoping you stay home today. I'm doing a repair job this afternoon. May have to work past three."

"What for?"

"Well, I was thinking we could use some extra money to buy a new vehicle. Grandma's old car may not make it much longer."

"Ok, I'll ask my friend for a ride or take the school bus."

"You sure? If not, I'll cancel the job and pick you up."

"No, it's ok, I'll be fine."

"Do you want breakfast?"

"No, I can eat at school with my friend."

Henry grabbed his cap and keys. "You ready?"

"Yes."

Within days, Henry had abandoned his afternoon routine with Jenny. Inundated with renovation projects, he began feeling guilty for not being the parent Jenny deserved. He snuck in a beer or two whenever he felt overwhelmed and anxious. He felt like he had inherited one of his mother's worst qualities — that of an absent parent.

CHAPTER FORTY-NINE

Wednesday, October 16, 2002
(Five months later)

H enry arrived home late one evening, long after Jenny had gone to bed. Exhausted from working a long hour day, and no appetite for food, he forged himself into a comfortable spot on the sofa and fell fast asleep.

Sometime later that evening, Jenny walked into the living room to find Henry stretched out on the sofa.

She pulled on his shirt. "Dad, wake up."

His speech slurred as he stirred. "What? What did you say?"

"Dad, I'm talking to you."

Mentally, he couldn't think, and physically he couldn't move. Kept his head on the pillow, his eyes struggling to open.

Jenny stood and watched as he fell back into a deep sleep. She whispered, "I don't like you when you're like this."

This scene was becoming his new normal. The tireless hours of working, not getting enough sleep, combined with not eating well, were depleting him of energy, of life, of his relationship with his daughter.

By the end of the week, he couldn't function. He halted work on his projects and returned home early. The plan was to take a quick nap while he waited for Jenny to arrive from school, but that soon changed when he drifted into a deep sleep on the sofa.

Hours later, he opened his eyes to find the house in complete darkness. He called out, "Jenny."

No response.

Again he called out.

Perhaps Jenny was in her room asleep.

He knocked on her bedroom door. "Jenny you awake?"

No answer.

Instead of knocking again, Henry opened the door, peaked in, no sign of Jenny. His palms were feeling sweaty. A sign of his anxiety setting in. He felt his heart racing. And right as he was about to call on the phone for help, the front door burst open. It was Jenny.

"Dad, you're awake."

"Where have you been?"

"I came home from school. You were fast asleep on the sofa, so I went to my friend's house. Worked on some homework and then she invited me for dinner."

"Why didn't you leave a note or call?"

"I didn't think about it."

Henry's tone took a rather dark side. "Are you lying to me?"

"No."

Suspicion seeped through Henry's mind. He grabbed Jenny by the arm as she was about to walk away.

"Tell me the truth." He said.

"Ouch! Let go of my arm."

He pressed a little harder.

"Dad, what's wrong with you? I told you the truth. I'm not like your mom, who lied to you and didn't come back."

Henry released Jenny's arm.

"Look what you did! My arm is going to be bruised tomorrow!"

Jenny ran to her room, slamming the door behind her.

Henry ran after her, "Jenny, open the door, now!"

"Dad, stop it. What's wrong with you?"

Jenny leaped on the bed. In fear, she piled all the pillows on her.

Henry busted the door open and stumbled onto the foot of the bed. He yelled at her, "Never close the door on me! This is my house!"

Jenny put her hands up. "Don't hurt me!"

"I would never think of hurting you. Please don't close the door on me again. Do you understand?"

She whispered, "Yes."

"I didn't hear you."

"Yes."

He walked across the hallway and slammed the door shut to his room. His heart was racing. Take a deep breath. Take a deep breath. Not since his youth had he experienced such anger. Take a deep breath. Take a deep breath. Focus. Count the stripes on the bedsheet, count the knobs on the dresser. Focus. Count buttons in the jar.

Henry tilted his head back, looking at the ceiling. He cried, "I'm an idiot. What did I just do?" He whispered, "I'm sorry, I'm so sorry, I didn't mean, oh God, help me." He wiped his face. "God, where are you? I need you. My heart, it's not in the right place." He grabbed the glass lamp sitting on the nightstand and threw it against the wall, shattering it into pieces. He dropped to the floor. "Where are you? Can you hear me? I don't know how to do this anymore."

CHAPTER FIFTY

Thursday, October 17, 2002
(The following day)

Morning came too soon and with it a sickly feeling in the air. Henry entered the living room to find Jenny holding her backpack to her chest. Hair wet from a morning shower, she wore a long sleeve shirt and jeans.

He adjusted his cap. "Do you want breakfast?" He asked.

She shook her head.

He grabbed his keys from the coffee table as he made his way to the door, with Jenny trailing behind.

They made the drive to school in silence since neither one had any desire to talk to the other after last night's trying situation.

When they arrived, it was Henry who spoke with a broken voice, "I didn't mean to hurt you last night."

Ignoring his words, Jenny slammed the door to the car as hard as she could.

He sniffed back the tears. He would try to talk to her after school.

Hours later, Henry was finding it hard to stay focused on work as the morning dragged into mid day. Thoughts of Jenny drifted in and out of his mind for a good part of the early morning. He eventually cut his day short and went home to fix her bedroom door. Afterwards, he sat and waited for Jenny to arrive from school.

She entered the door at half past four, ignoring Henry altogether, as she made her way straight to her room, slamming the door shut.

He could feel the tension building up around his neck. How was he going to fix this? The sitting around waiting for the situation to resolve itself was making him feel anxious. Take a deep breath. Take a deep breath. Minutes later, he glanced at the clock. Perhaps he should wait and talk to her later? Or maybe go try to talk to her now? He decided on the latter.

He knocked on the door. "Jenny, we have to talk."

"I don't want to talk. Leave me alone."

"No Jenny, I can't leave it like this. It's hurting us both."

"Leave me alone!" She yelled.

"Please, open the door."

The doorknob jiggled.

Henry opened the door slowly.

Jenny stood as far away from him as she could. She had changed into a pair of shorts and a short sleeve t-shirt. The bruises on her arm were visible.

He wanted to tell her he was sorry for his ignorance. Would it do much good, though?

Her broken voice whispered, "Are you going to hurt me again?"

Henry could see the hurt in her green eyes.

He responded, "No, no, last night was a mistake. I felt scared, worried you were out there alone and something might happen to you."

She cried out, "Look at my arm, it hurts!"

"I know it hurts. And I take full responsibility. I'm an idiot for not knowing how to handle the situation. This was exactly the thing I feared. I thought working these extra jobs to make more money to buy you stuff and to buy myself a truck would be ok. I assumed you would come straight home from school. Lock the door and stay put. Should have known better. And look what's happened? Right when I thought we were becoming a family."

"I hate you!"

"Please, no, no, don't say that. You're angry with me right now."

"Get out of my room."

"I will make it better. I promise."

She picked up the shoe on the floor and threw it at him. "Get out!" She yelled.

He closed the door behind him. He knew what she was feeling, because he, too, was living with it every day. And because of his actions, or lack thereof, he feared losing her. She was all the family he had.

Somehow, someway, affliction and misery had made their way back into Henry's life. He retreated to his room, slamming the door shut. Turned to the mirror. All he could see was an image of failure. He touched his face. He looked thin and haggard. Gray strands in his hair were aging him much too fast. Anger spilled out, toppling everything on the dresser. Hung his head over, crying, he whispered, "Mom you were right when you said I had been born good for nothing."

CHAPTER FIFTY-ONE

Monday, September 27, 2004 (Two years later)

H enry's promise to do better didn't last very long. Living under the same roof proved to be quite a challenge for both Henry and Jenny. Neither one felt comfortable in each other's presence anymore. Jenny spent most of her time away at a friend's house, while Henry made it a point to keep himself focused on his work by working long hours.

Today Henry found it difficult to stay on task and work a full day. Building a room addition in 100-degree weather had left him spent. He gathered up his tools, cleaned the sawdust off his cap. A cold beer came to mind. In fact, it could very well take the edge off and help him relax. After wrestling with his thoughts for several minutes, he dismissed the idea and got on the road and headed home. The thought set in again when he drove past an icehouse with people sitting around a picnic table enjoying their afternoon refreshments. Drove past a second icehouse. At the third icehouse, he made a stop. One beer couldn't hurt. Jenny didn't have to know. Besides, she would probably be at her friend's house. What harm could one beer do, anyway?

Henry arrived home well after dark, stumbling, trying to get inside the front door.

He called out, "Jenny!"

The moment she heard him, she closed the door to her room and locked it. She was tired. School homework had taken most of her energy and right now, she was in no mood to face her father.

His voice grew louder. "Jenny, where are you?"

Jenny grew angry the moment she heard the tone in his voice. He was drunk. She wanted to run out of the house, never to return, but feared he would catch up to her and now his footsteps were outside her bedroom door. Her eyes scanned the room, looking for a place to hide. But where?

He banged on the door, yelling, "Jenny, open the door!"

Bathroom seemed her best option. Curling into a fetal position inside the bathtub, she pulled the shower curtain, covering her mouth, hoping he couldn't hear her breathing.

The bedroom door flew open.

Jenny's eyes filled with tears.

Henry became overwhelmed with emotion as he whispered, "Jenny, I'm sorry. I'm so sorry I hurt you. Jenny, where are you? I love you. Jenny, you're all I have." He wiped his face and continued, "That day I hurt you. It was an accident. I didn't mean to do it. Please Jenny, where are you? I'm sorry. It's been two years. Please, you have to forgive me."

Henry reached for the knob on the bathroom door. Jenny clenched her teeth and closed her eyes shut.

He pulled the door open.

She was sure he would pull the shower curtain and it would be the end of her. Instead, he collected himself and made his way out of the bedroom and headed towards the kitchen.

He needed to drown his emotional suffering in something. Pulled open the refrigerator; eggs, milk, ham and beans, nothing appealed to him. A heated anger set in, forcing him to slam the door shut.

Jenny's legs and arms were feeling cramped from being crunched up in the bathtub for so long. She wanted to go see what was going on, but feared what he might do to her; she chose to wait until later.

Once the house fell silent, Jenny decided she

would risk getting out of the bathtub to stretch her body. Tiptoed out of her room and into the hallway to find it quiet. Inside Henry's room; it too was quiet. Her heart racing as she made her way through the hallway and into the living room. There was an odor circulating the room. She turned to see Henry stretched out on the sofa. His snoring meant he was in a deep sleep, at least for the time being. His clothes were wet and looking as if he had spilled something on them. Tears streamed down her cheeks. She couldn't believe the man she recognized and loved as her father in such a short time could not overcome his past. Would his anger still be present tomorrow? And would he hurt her again? She felt scared for her life. It was time to get out, and fast.

She picked up the phone and dialed a friend who agreed to pick her up.

Fearing Henry might stir at any moment, she quickly stuffed whatever clothes she could into her backpack. Wiped her tears as she took one last look at her room when she noticed the picture frame of her mom sitting on the dresser. She couldn't leave it behind. Quietly, she made her way through the hallway, reaching the front door. After taking a deep breath, she stepped out into the dark. With no plan, she wondered what her tomorrow would look like.

Within minutes, a red car emerged from the shadows. A tall and slender man with a cigarette in his mouth stepped out. He hugged Jenny. His hush tone made him likable on the spot.

"So what happened?" He asked her.

Jenny cried, "My father, he's messed up. I'm afraid of him."

"I'm sorry."

She wiped her teary face; "I can't live with him anymore."

"Hey, it's ok. You can stay with me as long as you need to. Don't cry anymore, you're messing up those pretty green eyes." He wiped her teary face and helped her get into the car. They disappeared into the shadows.

CHAPTER FIFTY-TWO

Tuesday, September 28, 2004
(The following day)

The morning sun filtered through the living room window. Henry stirred. He was feeling the ill effects of the night before. His head was throbbing. He licked his lips, swallowed, only to discover a vile taste on his tongue. His entire body felt weighted. He kept still, hoping to regain some form of strength to sit up until he discovered a strange odor circulating the room. Looking around the room, he saw nothing. Glanced at his clothes, they were sticky and damp, but from what? What had he done the night before? Touched his head, couldn't remember. Why couldn't he remember?

He ran to Jenny's room. The door was hanging from the top hinge. Had he busted the door again? Why couldn't he remember? His attention turned to the room. Everything appeared to be in its place except for her backpack. It was missing. She must have gone to school. At that moment, he wanted to run out the door to go look for her, but then realized he had to clean up first.

Henry arrived at the school mid morning to inquire of Jenny's attendance, only to be informed she was not in class.

He drove past his home twice before realizing where he was. His mind was in complete chaos. Where could she be? He couldn't think. His onslaught headache was keeping him from thinking clearly. Maybe if he called the police. If Jenny came walking through the front door at any moment, she might be angry with him for not trusting her. He called Alvin instead.

"Alvin."

"Hi Henry."

"It's Jenny." Henry whispered.

"What's wrong with Jenny?" Alvin asked.

Henry's voice broke. "I can't find her."

"What happened?"

"I came home last night. She wasn't home, and now this morning when I woke up, she wasn't in her room. I don't know if she came home last night."

"Have you called the police?"

"No, not yet."

"I'm on my way."

A short time later, Alvin walked through the front door, "What's that smell?"

"I puked on my clothes. I ended up sleeping on the sofa last night, so now it's all over the sofa."

"What happened Henry?" Alvin asked.

Henry scratched his head. "I came home drunk last night. That's what happened!"

"Henry, you've got a serious problem."

"Yeah, I know."

"And Jenny? You checked her room to see if anything is missing?"

"The only thing I noticed missing was her backpack. I thought she was going to school, so I drove to the school a while ago to see if she was in class. The front office told me they counted her absent."

"Ok, then we need to call the police and report her missing."

"I can't remember anything from last night. What am I going to tell them?"

Alvin grabbed the phone. "I'll call. Because if we don't, no telling what might happen to her."

When Alvin completed the call, he came back to sit and wait with Henry. He studied his friend for a moment and then spoke, "They're sending an officer over to talk to you."

Henry ignored him. He pulled out a cigarette instead.

"Since when do you smoke?"

"Since right now. I'm feeling anxious and now my hands are getting sweaty. If I can't drink, then I need something else to calm me down."

"I'm so sorry."

"For what? Jenny?"

"Sorry for what you've had to go through in life. All because of your mother."

Henry stared at his shoes. "Yeah, after all this time, you would think I would be healed by now. It's been a lifelong battle to get over the emotional trauma I suffered because of her indifference towards me. She would kick me around. Tell me I was the ugliest thing she had ever seen." He wiped his face with the back of his hand. "The sad thing is, I can't hate her. My heart still loves her, even after all these years."

"Henry, I don't understand why you didn't reach out to me before your situation got out of control. You know I'm here to help you."

"I had it under control and then this thing with Jenny. I just lost it."

"God can help you get back on track."

"I'm not in any condition to hear about God right now."

"Henry, this thing is more than just about you. It's about your daughter too."

Henry puffed at his cigarette and then smashed it in a cup. "Yep, a daughter who now hates me."

"I don't get it."

"You don't get what?" Henry asked.

Alvin leaned back in the chair and crossed his arms, "How is it you can hear the word of God in church and you walk out believing in him? And yet you refuse to obey his word. Life could be so much better for you if you just obeyed."

"Alvin, please don't go there."

"I'm sorry, but if I don't, I'm not being the man God wants me to be."

A knock on the door cut off the conversation.

Alvin opened the door to see a woman dressed in a police uniform. She gave Alvin and Henry a suspicious look. After questioning Henry for about thirty minutes, touring the house, taking photographs and notes, she requested Henry drive to the police station for further questioning.

CHAPTER FIFTY-THREE

Wednesday, September 29, 2004

Within twenty-four hours of Jenny's disappearance, Henry filed a missing person's report. Television news stations began running segments for Jenny's disappearance. Police conducted several area searches throughout the city, but no signs of Jenny surfaced anywhere. The earth somehow, someway had swallowed up Jenny's existence.

Hours of waiting to hear of Jenny's whereabouts would eventually turn into days, then into weeks, and ultimately months.

Thursday, November 17, 2005

As the days came and went, Henry deemed all hope lost of ever seeing his daughter again, until one day he received a telephone call.

"Hello." Henry answered.

"Speak to Mr. Henry Odin."

"I'm Henry Odin."

"This is Officer Gabe Kusik. I'm calling with the Department of Missing Persons."

Henry closed his eyes, took a deep breath. A sudden weakness seeped through his body, causing him to fear the worst. He pulled out a chair and sat down.

The officer continued, "A girl fitting your daughter's description came into the emergency room at Mercy Hospital earlier today."

Silence.

"Mr. Odin, are you there?"

"Yes." Henry whispered.

"We need you to come to Mercy Hospital."

"Is she okay?"

"I'm sorry, Mr. Odin, I can't discuss anything more over the phone."

"I'm on my way."

The hospital was a distance away. That meant Henry had time to collect his thoughts and think about what he was going to say to Jenny when he saw her. He couldn't wait to see her green eyes. He wanted to hug her and tell her he loved her. But what if she didn't want to see him? No, he couldn't think like that right now. He pushed the negative thoughts away. He needed to believe it was all going to be ok from on.

Anxiety set in the moment he drove into the hospital parking lot. Take a deep breath. Take a deep breath. He wiped his face as he approached the reception desk for information, only to be told to sit and wait for the doctor.

Moments later, a doctor pushed his way through the glass doors, making his way towards Henry. An officer trailed behind. Henry kept his eyes on the doctor, all the while rubbing his sweaty hands over and over.

"Mr. Odin?" The doctor asked.

"Yes." Henry replied.

"Have a seat, please."

The doctor spoke, "We admitted a girl this morning. She appears to be fifteen or sixteen years of age. Came in terrible shape. With a rapid heartbeat, problems breathing, her blood pressure was low."

"I want to see her. Where is she?"

"Yes, but first you must know she is very ill. She may not pull through."

"What?"

"We discovered in examining her she was suffering from a hemorrhage."

"I don't understand."

"By the time she arrived here, she had already lost a great deal of blood."

"But how?"

"She was pregnant."

Henry felt a weakness seep through his entire body again, fueling even more anxiety.

"And the baby?" He asked.

"The baby is fine. We delivered the baby by c-section."

Take a deep breath. Take a deep breath. "Why didn't someone call me earlier?"

The officer interrupted, "The girl only gave her first name. We try to work on these cases as fast as we can, but sometimes we take a while to find the right parents. I'm sorry."

"I need to see her."

"She's sedated, so she may not respond to you." The doctor said.

Fear led me by the hand as I walked into the room. Lights were dim. A dull color of grey covered the walls from top to bottom. Much like my past and now much like my present. The quiet in the room felt suffocating. I approached the bed. Take a deep breath. Take a deep breath. I stared at the body of the young girl lying on the bed. Her hair cut short and dyed in different shades of purple and blue. I tucked a strand of hair so I could see her face in the dim light. It was the same angelic face I'd grown to love and care for in a short period. Disguised underneath the heavy makeup was her cute nose. Dried up tears were still evident on her cheeks, probably from the excruciating pain she had suffered. On the inside of her left arm was a tattoo in the form of a tiny flower. The inscription below the tattoo read Lily. Perhaps it meant something. Wiped my eyes. Wanted to pick her up, hold her and take her home with me. Wanted another chance to make it right. I couldn't understand how life had gone so wrong. My fifteen-year-old daughter was on the verge of dying and leaving behind a newborn baby. Jenny didn't deserve to be in that bed. I did. It was my fault for not having been the parent I should have been. If there was ever a time, I needed God to come through with a miracle; this was the time. But would God even hear my pleas?

At that moment, the door to the room flew open, forcing Henry to wipe his tears. The nurse said, "Mr. Odin, I brought you a glass of water. You know you can stay as long as you want. If you need anything, press the red button on the wall. Any nurse will assist you."

"The baby." Henry's broken voice whispered.

The nurse smiled and said, "I can bring her to you."

"Her?" Henry's voice cracked.

"You have a beautiful granddaughter."

Take a deep breath. Take a deep breath.

Minutes later, the nurse returned with a bassinet on wheels. Henry choked on his cries the moment he saw the tiny newborn swaddled in a pink blanket.

"Mr. Odin, would you like to hold her?"

He nodded.

"I'll be back in fifteen minutes." The nurse said.

Henry looked down at the tiny bundle in his arms. She had a head full of messed up hair and the same cute nose as Jenny. For the next fifteen minutes, he talked to Jenny about the baby and how she needed to get better so they could all go home and be a family. Minutes later, an alarm brought his conversation to a halt. It was coming from the machine next to Jenny's bedside. A doctor and his nursing staff rushed into the room, forcing Henry to step aside. He feared the worst.

Several hours later, exhausted and emotionally spent, Henry left the hospital. The security guard in the parking lot bid him goodnight, but he couldn't hear him. He looked around the parking lot. Cars were driving by. People were engaging in conversation. He still couldn't hear anything. There was a strange silence idling around him.

Wrestling with his emotions, he got into his car. "It's my fault! My fault! I did this to her!" Fear turned into anger as he drove away. The streetlights on the road became a blur; the highway ahead had no destination. He looked at the speedometer, then at the road ahead. He gripped the steering wheel. Maybe if he sped up fast; he could go be with Jenny and never be apart from her again. Then the baby came to mind. Henry hit the steering wheel and slowly took his foot off the accelerator. Couldn't do it. Right thing to do was to take the next exit off the highway and head home instead.

CHAPTER FIFTY-FOUR

The moment I walked through the front door, I headed straight to the one room in the house where I could still feel connected to Jenny. It was her room. I touched the door. My muffled cries echoed throughout the house. I wanted her back home, where she belonged.

Pushed open the door, closed my eyes for a moment, trying to imagine her presence in the room. It was no use. She was gone.

I scanned the room, looking for something of hers that might help me calm down. There was Jenny's dirty sneaker, peaking from underneath the bed. Topped on the pink dresser were all her girly things. Scattered throughout the room pictures of her friend and herself in happy times. I glanced at the walls, remembering how Jenny and I argued about splattering various colors on the walls. In the end, Jenny and her friend secretly painted a wall to her liking, decorating it with posters. A hairbrush, a pair of jeans on the bed along with a stuffed bear, gave the bed an unkempt look. Became overwhelmed with emotion. I closed the door.

Felt the silence returning. This time it

appeared plastered all over the walls; growing louder and louder, closing in on me, making me feel trapped, suffocated. Couldn't breathe. I turned from room to room, trying to catch my breath, but it wasn't helping. Had to get out of the house. Where was the door? Why couldn't I find the door? My chest felt tight and weighted. Was I having a heart attack? Ran out the back door, clenching my shirt to my chest, gasping for air over and over until my breathing returned to normal.

I needed help, but who was going to help me? I'd cut communication with everyone, including God. Surely God could no longer hear me.

I felt tired, so tired. The emotional baggage I'd been carrying around in my mind, in my heart since I was a boy, had taken a toll on my life. It was time to do something. The thought of taking my life into my own hands crossed my mind for a moment. And would anyone care if I was gone? No. No one would care.

Covered my face, trying to muffle my cries, when out of nowhere a gentle breeze appeared, calming my body, my anxiety. The crying stopped. Oh, how I needed mercy to step in and save me at this moment.

I recalled a scripture Alvin had given me years back: "Have mercy on me, oh God, wash me thoroughly from mine iniquity, cleanse me from my sin."

Put my hand to my chest and whispered, "God, if you can hear me, help me. I need peace in my heart right now." Take a deep breath. Take a deep breath. "Come, show me what to do with my life. I'm ready to be the man you want me to be."

CHAPTER FIFTY-FIVE

The next day, Henry was back at the hospital. This time it was to see his granddaughter, who had yet to be named. He found a quiet spot in a vacant room next to the nursery so he could hold her and talk to her. He learned to bottle feed her and even changed his first diaper.

A short time later, a nurse returned to check on Henry and the baby. "Mr. Odin, you doing ok?" she asked.

Take a deep breath. Take a deep breath. "Yes, everything is fine."

"You have a visitor."

Henry glanced up to see a familiar face. It was Becca.

"Hi." She said.

He cleared his throat. "Hi there."

"How are you doing?"

Henry shook his head, "Not well."

"I'm so sorry about Jenny."

He shrugged his shoulders and said, "I messed up."

"You are not the only one who's messed up."

He responded. "I would ask you, but I'm thinking you're not ready to talk about it."

"No, no, I'm not. Maybe someday." She pulled a chair next to Henry and said. "She's beautiful. Just like her momma and her grandpa."

Feeling giddy on the inside, Henry smiled back at Becca. As much as he wanted to have a relationship with Becca, it wasn't the right time. In fact, there was never a right time. And now he had his hands full with trying to raise a newborn. He dismissed the thought and went back to thinking of the baby in his arms.

"Have you named the baby?" Becca asked.

"I was thinking Lily."

"Why Lily?"

"I think the name Lily may have had a special meaning for Jenny."

"It's a pretty name."

"So, are you in town visiting your parents?"

"Actually, I took a job with city parks and recreation."

"Here?"

"Yes, I'm moving back home."

Henry's eyes lit up.

Becca noticed the change in his expression. She added, "It's time I took responsibility for some things in my life. It's also time I think about settling down, too."

He took a deep breath. The words settle down were magic to his ears. Something he'd been craving his entire life. He wanted someone in his life to love. Someone with whom he could keep a messy house and grow old with. But the chances of that happening at his age were practically impossible. His eyes teared up.

CHAPTER FIFTY-SIX

Sunday, December 19, 2005 (one month later)

At thirty-seven, Henry settled into a new role in life, that of a grandparent. He stared at baby Lily in his arms. She was falling asleep feeding on her bottle. Anytime he attempted to pull the bottle away, she would start crying. A sign her personality was taking shape. He took a deep breath and gave her back her bottle, hoping this time she would sleep longer than thirty minutes. A short time later, their quiet time ended with an unexpected knock on the door.

It was Becca. Take a deep breath. What was she doing here? I wanted to see her. But like right now? I hadn't even changed out of my night clothes or washed my face.

"Hi." She said.

I never gave much thought to the word hi until Becca began using it. She gave it an entirely fresh feeling. That certain feeling that stirs the heart. Take a deep breath. She stood at the door with several bags in hand, looking at me awkwardly. I came back into the present when she said I bought you some things. I let her in. She walked past me, leaving behind her light floral scent. She was wearing an oversized sweater, some cut-off shorts, and those stupid cowboy boots of hers. Take a deep breath. I decided I would reserve those boy girl thoughts for later. Right now, I needed to think clearly so I could find out what her intentions were.

"So what's in the bags?" Henry asked as he put Lily in her bassinet.

"Well, I thought I might be a good neighbor."

Henry laughed, "Becca, you don't even live in the area."

She laughed too, "So what! Friends can visit each other, right?"

Henry cleared his throat, "I think you and I are past the childhood friendship. Don't you think?"

She fought back the tears blurring her eyes.

"Why do you fight it?" Henry asked.

"You have no idea what I've been through."

"Well then, talk to me. Sit down. I have all the time."

Becca's voice broke. "I was eighteen. I wanted to go away to college. Show my parents I could be responsible and grown up. My parents said ok. They bought me all this stuff for my dorm. They drove for miles to get me settled into my little room. My first night there, a student raped me. That night, my life changed forever. When I found out I was pregnant, I wanted to go out and get an abortion. I felt dirty, violated and robbed of my happiness. I wanted to rid myself of the dirtiness in my body. Yet my parents still wanted me to have the baby. I fought with them over and over about it. They didn't understand. It was my body. My choice. In the end they made me have the baby. When the baby was born, I refused to look at it. Refused to hold it. Wanted nothing to do with it. My parents took the baby and raised it as their own. I got myself back into college, got my career going. I took jobs out of state so I wouldn't have to be close to family or the baby. Over the years, I started coming around, but always kept my heart at a distance. I wasn't ready to accept Jonah in my life, and certainly not ready to accept a relationship with a man in my life until you showed up."

Henry sat back on the sofa and said. "I knew there was something there. I thought maybe you had been married and gone through a divorce and your parents were helping you out with Jonah. Never imagined you having that kind of experience."

Becca wiped her face, but it was no use. The tears kept spilling. She added, "That night when you and I met at the bar, it was the first time in my life I felt safe around a man. When you took me in your arms and held me on the dance floor, it felt like someone had cleaned me of my past. I wanted that moment to last forever. I went from being your childhood friend to being the grown-up girl in your arms." Becca whispered, "I fell in love."

Henry pulled Becca into his arms and held her for as long as time would allow them the moment.

CHAPTER FIFTY-SEVEN

Saturday, July 22, 2006 (Several months later)

Henry arrived at the baseball field with Lily in a stroller. Seated in the stands, Becca waved when she saw them approaching. Minutes later, Alvin and Jeanie arrived, too. With everyone seated, Jonah and his team were ready to play ball. Families in the stands cheered as each team tried their best to score. In the end, it was Jonah's skilled pitching that kept the other team from scoring. Ultimately, Jonah's team walked away with the trophy.

Henry and the Beard family celebrated after the game by going to the local pizza eatery. Once there, everyone took turns holding Lily. When it came time for Becca to hold Lily, Henry knew right there and then it was time. He smiled at her. She smiled back.

Take a deep breath. Take a deep breath. He began, "Becky, you were my childhood friend. Over time, you've become the grown-up girl in my arms. Every time I look into those blue eyes of yours, I fall in love with you all over again. I want to marry you and keep a messy house with you. I want to grow old with you."

By this point, Becca was no longer smiling, she was crying. "You love me? You really love me?" She asked.

Take a deep breath. Henry pulled a chair next to Becca, wiped her teary eyes, and said, "I wouldn't be giving you this ring if I didn't."

Becca inched closer to Henry as she whispered the three most important words his heart longed to hear. "I love you."

Chapter Fifty-Eight

Friday, August 22, 2008 (two years later)

H enry finally felt as if he was on track to have the life he'd always wanted. He had married his childhood friend Becca. Together, they learned how to parent Jonah and Lily. Becca learned to cook almost anything the family requested of her. Including the sausage patties Jonah loved so much as well as the chocolate chip pancakes with the smiley face Lily enjoyed. But it was the eggs she couldn't get quite right for Henry. They required a special touch. Perhaps it was the spices or maybe the cheese she wasn't getting right. Nevertheless, everyone seemed happy in the Odin household.

Henry worked tirelessly for an entire year, renovating his house for his new family. He even added an extra bedroom for Jonah and his dog. Today, he was putting the finishing touches on Jenny's old room.

Lily was excited to see her new room; holding

on to her two favorite dolls, she ran in, stopped mid center. Her fresh eyes looked around and blurted out, "Pretty."

Henry took her by the hand. "Yes, it's pretty. You like it?"

She nodded.

Henry painted the walls in a beautiful soft shade of lemon yellow. Daisy print curtains identical to the handmade quilt Jeanie and Becca had made for the bed dressed the windows rather nicely.

Lily's eyes danced with excitement.

"Lily, go look around." Henry ushered her around.

She ran to the painted rainbow by the corner window.

"Do you like it?"

She nodded.

Henry pointed to the other side of the room. "And over in that corner is a playhouse where you can play with your dolls."

Lily darted in that direction. Pecked inside the playhouse, and then glanced back at Henry.

He noticed the distressed look on her face. "What's wrong Lily?"

"To."

"Try Lily. Come on, honey. Say it."

Lily stood there looking at Henry until the word spilled out.

"Toys." She said.

"You like the toys?"

She nodded.

She then made her way to the bed. "Bed." She said

"Just for you."

She picked up the picture frame on the nightstand.

Henry scooped her up in his arms. "That's your mom." He said.

"Ma."

"Yes, look, you have her smile, her green eyes."

Lily held the picture frame close to her heart.

He fought back the tears.

Her small fingers wiped his teary eyes. When she was done, she said, "Pa."

"Yes Lily, grandpa has tears in his eyes. He misses Jenny."

"Did I just hear you say you miss Jenny?" Becca came into the room looking fresh, her hair still damp from showering.

"Being in this room stirs up some feelings."

Henry put Lily down as Becca was coming around to give him a peck on the cheek.

"And it's perfectly ok to feel that way. It's all part of the healing process. I think Lily being in here will be good for you and for her."

Becca put her arm around him and kissed him again. It felt like happy therapy for Henry to have her hugs and kisses. Her light floral scent was irresistible. Her blue eyes were mesmerizing. He had no trouble letting go of his anxiety whenever she was around.

She sat on the floor to talk to Lily. "Lily, you like your pretty room?"

Lily nodded.

"You have the best grandpa ever. Come here. I need a hug."

Becca sat Lily on her lap. Played with her hair. Pecked her on the cheeks. "You are so sweet. I love you."

Henry stood back and watched Becca and Lily smother each other with kisses. Any stranger watching them from afar could easily assume they were mother and daughter because of the tender relationship between them.

Becca glanced up at Henry. "What's on your mind?"

"I was thinking about how good you both look together. You were meant to be in each other's lives."

Becca winked. "Think God may have had a plan all along when he put you and I together."

"I think so too. Couldn't imagine sharing my life with anyone else but you."

Becca gave Henry a side eye look. "That's not all that's on your mind, is it?" She asked.

He took a deep breath. "I'm thinking about

Lily's speech delay. I'm concerned. She's almost three and all we get from her are random words here and there. She can't seem to connect the words to make phrases or sentences."

"Don't get discouraged. The speech pathologist says her speech will come in when she's ready. It's a matter of time. Look how far she's come already. She's giving us some words here and there."

"Yeah, you're right. I need to learn to be patient."

"She's got the best therapy." Becca said.

Henry chimed in, "Speaking of therapy, the clinic called. They have a slot available for next week, but I have to work."

"I can take Lily."

He smiled at his wife. "So what's the trade?"

"I was thinking."

Henry knew that look all too well. Anytime she started her sentence in that manner, it meant she had a plan. He laughed. "So, where are we going?"

She laughed, "Wait a minute, I didn't finish the sentence."

"Honey, you don't have to. I think I know you pretty well by now."

"And that's why I love you. You get me."

"Every day. All day."

She laughed again, "Ok, so I was thinking, we could go to the family picnic the church is having this Saturday. Lily can run around with some of her friends. My parents can come along too. Jonah should be able to go, too."

"I think it's a great idea." Henry replied.

CHAPTER FIFTY-NINE

Saturday, August 23, 2008 (Following day)

The church picnic was well underway by the time Henry and his family arrived. Alvin and Jeanie took charge of setting up their family picnic table with all the delicious foods prepared the night before. Jonah played ball with a few of his friends before taking his small dog for a walk around the grounds. Henry and Becca took Lily to see her friends. Lily sported a new pair of sneakers, a pair of printed shorts and an orange top. Her eyes danced with excitement the moment she saw her friends.

By midday, Henry and the Beard family were all back at the picnic table, ready to enjoy a delicious meal, when Becca pulled a card out of her purse. She thought it the perfect moment to hand it to Henry.

Looking somewhat confused, Henry asked, "What's this?"

"Just read it."

Henry grew stiff in his chair. He opened the envelope to find a pretty card.

Inside the card Becca had written the words, "We are adding a new member to the Odin family."

Henry's eyes lit up. "Are we getting another dog?"

Becca threw her arms around him. "No, silly."

Henry teased, "Another chicken?"

"A baby!"

Henry whispered in Becca's ear, "Have I told you lately how much I love you?"

Becca giggled silly, "Every day. All day."

CHAPTER SIXTY

Wednesday, August 27, 2008 (Few days later)

All the happiness in Henry's world couldn't fix Lily's speech problem. Becca's last-minute field inspection at one of the local parks impeded her from taking Lily to her appointment today. That left Henry to rearrange his schedule so he would be the one to take Lily to the nearby clinic.

Lily gripped Henry's hand as they walked across the parking lot. Once inside, an assistant escorted Lily to an activity room while Henry remained in the lobby. He took a deep breath. He felt his anxiety returning as his thoughts traveled back in time. Thinking of his mom's disappearance and how his heart still had no closure on the matter. And then his thoughts shifted to Jenny and what trauma she might have suffered during her pregnancy resulting in Lily's speech problem. Then there was Becca, his sweet wife, pregnant with their first child. She filled their home, their lives with such joy and love. Thirty minutes later, a voice interrupted his thoughts.

"Mr. Odin?"

Henry glanced around to see the speech pathologist calling him.

Take a deep breath.

"Mr. Odin, I'd like to bring you back to the activity room so we can talk."

Henry drew his eyebrows in, "Everything ok?"

"Oh yes, sure. I need to go over Lily's progress with you."

Henry entered the room. Children were scattered throughout the room. Some appeared to be working on their speech with therapists, while others worked on different projects. Henry glanced around the noisy room, looking for Lily. The moment he saw her, his eyes teared up. She was sitting quietly in a corner of the room with a doll on one side and a box of crayons on the other side. Her small hands were busy sorting through papers. She took a crayon in her left hand, pressed hard on the paper until it broke. She picked up another crayon. The same thing happened again.

He tucked his emotions in his pocket and headed towards her. He smiled, "Honey, what are you doing?"

She kept coloring.

"Can grandpa help you color?"

Her green eyes glanced up at Henry. "Purple." She said.

"I like purple too." He responded.

He couldn't help but notice how green her eyes had become and how her facial features were resembling Jenny more and more each day.

She held up the doll to Henry. Shook her head. "Not broken." She said.

Henry's eyes teared up again. "That's right honey, the doll is not broken."

She held out her arms. A sign she was done and ready to be picked up.

He wiped his teary eyes. "You ready to go home?"

She nodded.

Just then, the speech pathologist joined Henry and Lily for a quick review. "Mr Odin, Lily is picking up communication with pictures very well. I read a book to her today. In a matter of minutes, she communicated the story through pictures. I'm so proud of her. As for her speech, she has added more words to her vocabulary. I also see she is connecting a couple of words here and there to make phrases. She is making good progress."

Take a deep breath. Take a deep breath. "That's great news. It does my heart good to hear that." Henry replied.

"Not to worry. Your granddaughter is very bright. It's only a matter of time."

"Thank you." Henry replied.

"Oh, and one other thing. I meant to ask your wife the last time she was here, but I forgot. You have any relatives attending therapy here, too?"

Henry looked at her, puzzled. "No. Why?"

"A patient who has been coming into our clinic for therapy asked about Lily's last name. She said she has a relative with the same last name. Thought maybe there might be a relation."

Henry felt a cold chill. His entire body stiffed up. He choked on his words. "Do you? I mean. Can you provide the name?"

"No, I can't, because it's private information. Anyway, don't worry about it. I'm sure the world is overpopulated with the Odin name, just like mine. You have yourself a good day. The receptionist up front will schedule your next appointment."

Henry drove through his street twice before realizing he had passed up his house. He couldn't think straight. His mind was racing with questions. Who was it? Could it be? Why now? And what kind of therapy was the person seeking? He walked through the front door with Lily. Take a deep breath. Take a deep breath. He felt his palms becoming sweaty. It was starting all over again. The anxiety he had worked so hard to rid himself of had returned. And with it, fear.

An hour later, Becca and Jonah arrived home to find Henry paralyzed in fear.

"What's wrong?" She asked.

"I'm not sure."

"Talk to me."

Take a deep breath. Take a deep breath. "The speech pathologist asked me this afternoon if I had any relatives coming into the clinic. I asked her why. She said they have a patient that has been coming in for therapy. That person asked about Lily and her last name."

"Did you get that person's name?"

"No, they can't release personal information."

"So, are you thinking it might be your mom?" Becca asked.

"I mean, who else? I don't have any other relatives with the name Odin other than my grandma."

CHAPTER SIXTY-ONE

Saturday, December 8, 2012 (Four years later)

Henry loaded up Christmas gifts into his new truck, and then headed back inside the house. "Lily, where are you? We don't have all day." He called out.

"Grandpa, I'm putting my shoes on."

He grabbed his cap, shoved a cookie in his mouth before Lily followed him out the door.

The drive to the children's home in the city was but twenty minutes. He remembered the home all too well. For most of his early childhood years, this home had been his haven of hope more times than he could count on his fingers. He was so thankful Mary Ann had been around to help him. In fact, she was still very much involved in helping the new generation of children in the community.

Henry took Lily by the hand as they walked up the well-manicured walkway and through the weathered door of the children's home. The lobby area looked deserted.

The receptionist came around the corner to greet them. "Mr. Odin, so nice to see you."

"Where is everyone?" Henry asked.

"Mary Ann is in a meeting with the staff and the children are outside playing."

"I'm dropping off gifts. They're tagged with names of the children."

"Thank you so much. You can place them under the tree. I'll let Mary Ann know you're here."

Henry nodded.

After placing the gifts under the tree, Henry and Lily stepped outside into the garden. He felt a gentle breeze chill his face; triggering memories of a scrawny eight-year-old boy arriving in the dark dirty and hungry. He choked back the tears, feeling grateful this place had existed back then for him and grateful it was still here for the other children. He shoved his hands in his pockets. Watched as the many children chased each other around the playground. He couldn't help but think; they all had a common thread in their stories - abandonment, neglect, and sometimes, even abuse.

His attention then shifted back to Lily, who had taken to playing with her dolls underneath the grand old tree. She loved her white sneakers but hated shoelaces. Much like someone else he knew.

"Hello Henry," Mary Ann hugged him, "It's so nice to see you."

"Everything ok?" He asked.

"Oh yes, I was just meeting with my staff to tell them about yesterday's board meeting. Looks like we have a new donor who is interested in contributing to the new addition."

"New addition for what?"

"I'm sorry. I thought I told you. We have been looking at creating more space so we can take in more children."

Henry glanced out at the playground. "I don't get it. Why would a parent give up on their kid?"

"I've been trying to figure that out for years. I look at these children and all I see is love. Isn't it what people want in their lives? Love?"

"You would think so."

Mary Ann shifted her attention back to Henry. "I saw the gifts under the tree. I can't thank you enough. The children will be so happy to know there is someone who cares."

"I brought you one too."

Mary Ann's eyes lit up. "For me? Can I open it now?"

"Sure."

She opened the box to find a sculpted angel made of wood. "I love it Henry. Did you make this?" She asked.

"I did. I've been making them since college. Over the years, I've gotten better."

"I have the perfect place for it." She placed it on the round table in the foyer. "There, so everyone can enjoy it. How is your family?"

"Becca is now working part time. She wants to focus more of her time on Sara and Lily. She's trying to make up for not being there for Jonah when he was young. And speaking of Jonah, he just got a job out of state."

"And how is Lily?"

"She's doing well too, talks non-stop now. Becca and I are running around trying to keep up with her many activities."

"Henry and your mother?"

"Nothing. I think maybe I should just close the door on that chapter of my life and keep my focus on my family."

"God has certainly blessed you."

Henry's voice cracked. "More than I could have hoped for."

Just then, Lily made her way back to Henry.

Henry wiped the dirt off her knees. "You ready to go?"

Happiness spilled over her cherubic face as she said, "Yes, grandpa."

Mary Ann tucked a strand so she could take one last look at Lily. After a bit, she regained her composure and said, "You be good for grandpa."

Henry's voice broke as he spoke. "I don't know if I ever told you how grateful I am in my heart that you were there for me when I was a kid. No telling where I might be now had you not cared or attempted to connect me with my grandma."

"Stop right there, Henry, otherwise I'm

going to cry, too. I'm just glad your story finally has a happy ending," Mary Ann wiped her teary eyes. "Now you two better get going. I'm sure you have a lot to do as I do here. I have children I need to find families for."

As soon as they settled into the truck, Henry asked Lily, "What would you like to eat?"

"Grandpa, I want a hamburger with ketchup."

"A hamburger! You just had a hamburger yesterday. And you want another one today?"

"She nodded."

"You're going to turn into a giant hamburger."

She broke out laughing, "Grandpa, you're funny."

Henry joined in her infectious laughter as they made their way to the restaurant.

"We should be there in about fifteen minutes." He said.

"Is that a long time, grandpa?"

"No, not really."

"Grandpa, we going on the mix up roads again?"

Henry held up two fingers. "Just two mix up roads."

Lily pulled her two dolls away from the window and sat back. "Okay, Grandpa."

Henry took a deep breath. Glanced over at Lily. Feeling grateful for having her in his life but also feeling regret for not having appreciated his daughter Jenny like he should have.

Chapter Sixty-Two

Tuesday, September 17, 2013
(Nine months later)

Becca and four-year-old Sara sat around the kitchen table when Henry and Lily walked through the front door with pizza boxes in hand. Henry picked up Sara. Pecked her on the cheek. "Did you have a good day with mama?" He asked.

Sara nodded.

Becca made a face.

"I didn't forget about you." He kissed his wife. "Did you miss me?"

She snuggled her nose in his and whispered, "I miss you like there is no tomorrow."

He took a deep breath and kissed her again.

Midway through dinner, Lily emptied her backpack of her school papers while speeding through her words with a lightning of enthusiasm.

"Did you have a good day at school?" Becca asked.

Lily responded, "I want to go sleep in the woods and help the sick people."

Becca and Henry looked at her in a surprising way, and then Henry asked, "What?"

"Grandpa, it's in this paper."

"Where did you get this paper?" Henry asked.

She held up her hands. "In school, grandpa. A lady told all the girls."

Henry glanced at the paper and then passed it on to Becca.

Lily tucked her hands under her chin. "Please, please."

Henry added, "I don't think we have time for another activity. Honey, look at the calendar. Your Tuesdays and Thursdays are very busy days. You have the astronaut program at school and then there is the children's choir you joined at church. We have practice for that, too."

Becca chimed in, "Well, wait. We might be able to figure something out."

Henry made a face.

Lily tugged at his sleeve. "But grandpa."

He read the paper again. "It says there is a club meeting on Saturday. That's just two days away."

"Grandpa, do you want me to be sad?"

Henry and Becca broke out laughing.

He couldn't deny her an opportunity to learn to do well in the community. He glanced over at Becca, who was smiling. "Okay, we'll go to the meeting just to see what it's all about."

Lily threw her arms around him. "I love you, grandpa."

He hugged her tightly. "And I love you too."

"Grandpa, can you buy me the hat too?"

"What hat?"

"The lady she showed us the clothes we have to wear. I want the hat."

He smiled. "The pizza is getting cold. We should finish eating first, then you can tell us all about the hat."

Settling into her chair for a slice of pizza, she replied, "Ok grandpa."

CHAPTER SIXTY-THREE

Saturday, September 21, 2013

S aturday morning barreled in with rain show-ers prompting Henry and Becca to change their minds about the meeting, but then dismissed the idea when Lily walked into the kitchen dressed and with a ray of sunshine on her face.

Becca nudged Henry. "We can't cancel. It will break her heart."

Lily looked at the calendar on the wall, and then back at Henry. "Grandpa, is today the meeting?"

Looking over his coffee cup, he said, "You didn't change your mind?"

"Grandpa, are we going?"

"Yes, we are, but it's still too early."

"I'm ready."

"How about breakfast first?" He asked.

"Pancakes with the little sausages, just like last time."

Becca whipped up some pancakes in no time for the family while Henry worked on cooking the delicious sausages.

Once morning settled into midday, the entire Odin family loaded up and headed to the meeting at the nearby school. Surprised by how many parents were in attendance to sign up their girls for the club, Henry and Becca felt an obligation to do the same, besides it would be great for Lily to learn to help others in the community.

Upon seeing the uniform, Lily could hardly contain her excitement. She jumped up and down. "Grandpa, is my hat in the bag? Can I have it?"

"Yes, it is, but you will have to wait until we get home."

"Can we go home now?"

"Home it is."

Two months into Lily joining the club, Henry and Becca also found themselves getting recruited to take part in activities. Cleaning the local community park seemed to fit the Odin family best because it allowed Lily and Sara to run around the park, picking up trash while playing tag until they were spent.

Helping package food in bags at the local food bank not so much fun. At times, Henry had to step in and remind Lily of her commitment to the club to which she would have a tendency to curl her lips and cross her arms. Perhaps the best part about joining the club was the camping trip the entire Odin family would take part in, but only after completing a few more activities.

CHAPTER SIXTY-FOUR

Saturday, November 16, 2013
(Two months later)

Henry picked up Lily from the senior assisted living facility where she and the other girls volunteered to help with a recreational event.

Once they settled in for the drive home, Henry asked, "Did you have a good time?"

She made a face.

"Did something happen?"

She shook her head.

"Then why the sad face?"

"Not right now, grandpa."

"Ok then, you tell me when we get home."

Feeling as if the drive home would take forever, Lily felt she could no longer wait, so she began spilling details of the event. "Grandpa, he ate the soap."

"Who ate the soap?" Henry asked.

"The man, he was sitting in the corner. I gave him the basket. He ate the soap."

Henry looked at Lily with a puzzling look, "He ate the soap?"

Lily nodded, "The lady, she took it away from him, and he yelled really loud. Grandpa I got scared."

"And then what happened?" Henry asked.

"I wanted to go home."

Henry tried to calm her emotional rise by telling her, "I think maybe the man might have been hungry, or maybe he couldn't see very well. That's why he picked up the soap, thinking it was food."

"I don't want to go back there again."

"I tell you what, next time, I will go with you."

"Really grandpa, you will go with me?"

"Yes."

"I love you, grandpa."

CHAPTER SIXTY-FIVE

Saturday, December 14, 2013
(Four weeks later)

H enry made good on his promise. Four weeks later, he accompanied Lily and the other girls to the senior assisted living facility, which was next door to a clinic Lily used to frequent for her speech therapy years ago.

The facility looked weathered, front porch with some pretty rocking chairs gave the place an appearance of an actual home. The landscaping looked somewhat well manicured. A variety of pretty flowers aligned the walkway leading up to the front door. Dressed on the yellow walls in the lobby area were pretty landscaping prints. A petite woman came around the corner to greet the group of girls and then led them to the recreational area where everyone was already situated for their afternoon activities. Henry decided he would stay back and observe while Lily and the other girls worked with the group of seniors to make paper flowers. The art project took but thirty minutes.

Afterwards, the girls scattered around the room, helping with other activities.

Lily held in her hands two extra flowers. She asked Henry, "Grandpa, I still have two flowers."

Henry glanced around the room. "Well, let's find two people who didn't get flowers." He pointed, "Look, go give one to the man who is reading the book in the corner. And it looks like the lady in the wheelchair over by the window didn't get one either. Give her the last flower."

Lily handed the man the flower and then returned to Henry's side.

Henry hugged her, "Don't be afraid Lily, I'm right here; go give the lady the flower."

Lily approached the lady again and asked, "Would you like a flower?"

The nurse chimed in, "Sweetie, I don't think she can hear you like that, here let me turn the chair around so you can talk to her."

Lily stared at the lady, with the pretty pink gown and the matching slippers. Her short grey hair styled back. Her wrinkly dry skin seemed to indicate she might be eighty-years-old or more. She looked thin and frail sitting in her wheel-chair. Her eyes were closed. A sign she might be taking a nap.

Lily extended the flower to her again. "Hi, would you like a flower?"

Startled by Lily's small voice, the lady opened her eyes and said, "What do you want?"

Lily tried again. "It's a flower for you."

The lady squinted her eyes. "I can't see it. Come closer."

Lily moved a bit closer.

The lady cupped Lily's hands in hers. "Your little hands are so warm." She studied Lily's facial features. "Your eyes are so green; they have a happy light in them. I used to have eyes just like yours, but as I got older, the happy light disappeared."

Lily remained quiet.

The lady continued, "What is your name?"

"Lily."

"Your mommy picked a pretty name for you."

"I don't have a mommy."

"Then who is taking care of you?"

"My grandpa."

"Your grandpa?"

Lily pointed towards the door. "He's over there." She said.

Henry had perched himself by the doorjamb, keeping an eye on Lily but also watching how the rest of the girls provided helping hands to the aging group of people struggling to engage in activities otherwise deemed essentially easy for those in the outside world. He became teary-eyed at the thought of some of them not having any family to care for them. And he wondered how many might be facing terminal illness? Whatever their stories, it was clear they were all being held behind the confinement of sterile walls, waiting day after day to close the last chapter of their lives. He wiped his eyes.

The lady struggled to see Henry standing by the door. She said, "I can't see him. I need my glasses." She searched her pockets but couldn't find them.

"Are these it?" Lily asked as she picked them off the tray sitting next to the lady.

Carefully she put them on, turning her attention to Henry, who was still standing by the doorjamb. She spoke in a very thin and weakened voice, "He looks young to be a grand-pa." She squeezed her eyes shut and cried out, "It's hurting again."

Lily's distressed look prompted Henry to join her. "Something wrong Lily?" He asked.

"I don't know, grandpa."

Henry signaled to the nurse in the room, who was already headed in their direction.

"Everything ok?" she asked.

Henry spoke, "I think the lady may be in some pain."

The nurse looked at her watch and then at the lady. "Ms. Harding, it's not time for your pill yet. I'll have to talk to the doctor about getting you something stronger to make you more com-fortable. I'll be back in a moment."

The lady in the wheelchair took Henry's

hand and held on to it tightly. "The pain, it hurts everywhere. I'm living in hell."

"I'm so sorry. What is it you're suffering from?" Henry asked her.

"I have stomach cancer. I think a few months ago, or was it yesterday?" She looked out the window. "In this place, I don't know what day it is anymore." She lowered her head, rubbed her hands. A few moments later she tilted her head back, "I can't, I'm hurting. Where's the nurse? I need something."

Henry looked around the room, hoping the nurse was on her way back.

Tears filled the lady's eyes as she glanced over at Henry and then back at Lily. "The doctor said the cancer is everywhere." Her weak voice whispered, "He told me I can die any day."

Minutes later, the nurse came back, rushing into the room. "I'm so sorry it took so long. I couldn't find the person with the key to unlock the dispensing room. Here you go Ms. Harding. The doctor is adding some extra pain medication to your chart to make you more comfortable. Now, if you like, I can take you back to your room so you can rest."

She took the pills with the cup of water and then signaled the nurse to go away. "No, I want to stay here. The pill will work in a few minutes."

Lady turned to Henry again, "And you? What is your name?"

"Henry."

"You have a last name, Henry?"

"Odin."

She repeated the name slowly, "Henry Odin." Her eyes studied his face with great interest.

Henry felt uncomfortable with her stare, almost as if she was trying to recall something or someone.

He cleared his throat. "Are you ok?"

She nodded.

Henry felt something familiar about her. Was it the eyes? The voice? A sudden chill came over him. This entire scene was making him feel uncomfortable.

Henry asked her, "I'm sorry, what did you say your name was?"

"I didn't, but I'll tell you because you seem like a nice person. It's Lena Harding."

"Do you have any family?"

"No family."

Lily interrupted, "Look grandpa my friends are leaving."

Before walking away with Lily, Henry said to the lady, "It was nice meeting you. I hope you can get some rest."

Henry walked Lily through the building and out the door as quickly as he could. He was feeling a sense of panic; he needed to get some air. Once outside, he took a seat on a rocking chair, hoping to calm the panic feeling he was sensing. Take a deep breath. Take a deep breath.

Lily patted Henry on the shoulder. "Grandpa, are we going home?"

"Yes, but right now, I need to sit for a moment. Have to catch my breath."

She looked at him in her usual gentle demeanor, "Ok grandpa."

A short time later, Henry and Lily were on the road, headed home.

"Grandpa, you passed our house."

"What?"

"Grandpa, our house is that way."

"I'm sorry. I guess I'm tired."

"Grandpa, I'm hungry."

"We can eat something when we get home."

"Grandpa, are you mad?"

"No, honey. Grandpa is not feeling too well right now."

Becca was in the kitchen when Henry walked right past her without even saying a word. He poured himself a glass of water and forged himself into a spot on the sofa to think. Glanced over at Lily and Sara, who took to sorting through the coloring box. He gave them a tender smile as he tried to regain a form of composure without scaring them.

Lily put her small hand on his forehead. "Grandpa, you fill sick?"

"A little."

"I can pray for you, grandpa, so God makes you better."

Henry hugged his granddaughter, but then returned to his thoughts.

Moments later, he disappeared into the hallway. He needed to be alone to think and trace back to when he met the lady in the wheelchair. He needed to know more about her.

Becca stopped what she was doing in the kitchen. Washed her hands and went looking for Lily. "How was the event? Was it better this time?"

Lily nodded.

"And where did grandpa go?"

Lily shrugged her shoulders.

Becca peeked out the front window. Henry's truck was parked in its usual spot in the driveway. She searched the bedrooms on the opposite side of the house. Nothing. She headed to her bedroom. The door was closed. She pried the door open to find Henry sitting on the floor, leaning against the bed rail. He was crying.

Becca whispered, "What's happened? I've never seen you like this."

Take a deep breath. Take a deep breath. He choked on his words. "There was a woman in a wheelchair. She had my mom's eyes. When she spoke, it was as if my mom was speaking. It stirred up my past. Memories of my mom and her actions came back to haunt me. How she treated me. The seedy childhood I was stuck in. It's been over thirty years since she walked out the door and disappeared. And yet I still remember that afternoon as if it were yesterday. Crying out to her. Begging her not to leave me. Looking back, I think my heart may have known she planned not to return that night. The thing is, I still love her. I feel her in my heart every day. I haven't been able to let go." He rubbed his neck. He looked at his palms. "My palms are sweating." Take a deep breath. Take a deep breath. "I feel my anxiety returning."

Becca gently massaged his shoulder. "So, what do you want to do?"

"I think I need to return to see the woman in the wheelchair. I feel like she might have something to do with my past. The thing is, she said she has no family. And yet I feel drawn to her for some reason."

"Did you get her name?" Becca asked.

"She said her name was Lena Harding."

"Did your mom ever mention anyone by that name?"

"No. And I don't remember meeting her friends other than the man in the red car."

"When are you thinking you might want to go back to the facility?"

"I'm thinking Tuesday. It's the only day I don't have a lot going on."

"Would you like for me to come with you?"

"No. I think it's something I need to do for myself."

Becca kissed him softly. "Don't allow fear to get in the way of your faith."

He kissed her back. "I know. This time it's different."

CHAPTER SIXTY-SIX

Tuesday, November 26, 2013 (Few days later)

Tuesday could not have come fast enough for Henry, out of bed the moment daylight appeared through the window. He piddled around the kitchen a bit before sitting at the counter with his coffee. He'd hope to have a moment alone to collect his thoughts before everyone else began piling in for breakfast. However, all hope diminished minutes later when Becca walked in with Sara and Lily trailing behind.

"Grandpa, what are you doing?" Lily asked as she scooted a chair next to him.

Sara was not to be left behind either; she made herself comfortable on Henry's lap.

"Grandpa?" Lily asked again.

He squeezed her in with Sara. "Well, I was trying to collect my thoughts."

Becca made a face. "You seem to be doing a lot of that lately."

"I know, and I'm sorry. As soon as I figure out this thing at the senior facility today, I'm hoping everything will return to normal."

An hour later, Henry was ready to face the unknown, but first he had to drop Lily off at school.

"Have any of you seen my keys?" He asked.

"They are hanging by the door, grandpa."

"I guess I forgot."

"Wait, aren't you forgetting something else?" Becca asked.

He gathered Sara in his arms, kissed her on the cheek. He turned around, gave his wife a wet kiss.

"I love you." She whispered.

"And I love you. Every day, all day."

Chapter Sixty-Seven

(Same day, a couple of hours later)

After attending to some work related errands, Henry arrived at the senior facility by mid morning. He parked his truck. Sat back in his seat, reconsidering his entire plan to go inside and attempt to talk to the woman in the wheelchair. He hit the steering wheel and muttered something underneath his breath. He felt like an idiot. Why couldn't he just leave everything the way it was? Why drag his past back into his life and mess up his present? And then Becca and the girls came to mind. If he was ever to be the husband, the father, his family deserved to have; he needed to be free of the baggage still lingering in his heart. What he needed was closure to this thing that had haunted him for most of his life. He took a deep breath, wiped his teary eyes, and headed inside.

The receptionist asked, "Hello, can I help you?"

Henry stuttered, "I, I was here a few days

ago with my granddaughter and her friends. We met a lady. I think she said her name was Lena Harding."

"Yes, Ms. Harding."

"Can I visit with her?"

"Are you a relative?"

"It's a long story."

The receptionist looked at him suspiciously. "Are you on the visitor list?"

"No, I'm not."

"I'm sorry, Ms. Harding would have to approve you as a visitor."

The anxiety set in. He looked down at his palms. They were sweating again. He didn't know how to explain his situation. The obvious thing was to tell her the truth; otherwise he could be denied access to a visit with the lady. "I feel like she might be a relative." He said.

The receptionist made a phone call. She turned to Henry. "Someone will be with you in a moment."

Just as Henry was about to sit, the double doors opened. "Hello, I'm Dorothy Grimes. I manage the facility. How can I help you?"

"I, I was here yesterday."

"Yes, I remember you and your granddaughter."

"We met one of your residents. She's in a wheelchair. Her name is Lena Harding."

"Oh yes, Ms. Harding. She is a sweet lady, but very ill."

"I'd like to visit with her. Think she might be related to my mom."

"I don't understand."

Take a deep breath. Take a deep breath. "My mom disappeared years ago when I was young. Police never found her."

"And you think Ms. Harding might be your mother?"

"I don't know. Maybe she's related to my mom in some way."

The manager eyed Henry strangely. "Do you have pictures? Documents?"

"I have nothing. All I remember about her was that she had light brown hair, her eyes were green, and she had a distinct tone in her voice."

"Oh, goodness, that information won't be of much help. What about her name?"

"Her name was Liset Odin."

"Was that her maiden name? Married name?"

"Maiden name. My mom wasn't married."

"Well, I don't know what to tell you. This lady's name is Lena Harding."

Henry gave her a blank stare.

The manager stated, "When we admitted Lena Harding, she told us she had no family. I don't see how you can be a relative then."

His voice broke. "Is there any way you could

talk to her? Tell her I need to visit with her for a moment."

She studied his eyes; they had a look of desperation. She decided she would try to help him. "Let me go talk to Ms. Harding and see what she says. Please have a seat in the lobby. I'll be back."

The manager returned a short time later, and said, "She's agreed to see you."

Take a deep breath. Take a deep breath. "Did she say anything about me?"

"No, she didn't. She is sitting outside under her favorite tree, having her coffee. It has been her morning routine for over twenty years. I'll take you to see her now."

As they made their way through the hallway, the manager said to Henry, "I would like to ask you not to stress her with your story. Her health is in a very delicate stage."

"Yes, I know. She told me about it yesterday." Henry replied.

The moment they stepped outside, Henry felt his body tensing all over. He rubbed his hands, trying to keep them from sweating. Scared his uneven breathing might trigger a panic attack; he placed his hand over his chest in an effort to bring his breathing back to normal.

When they reached the tree, it was the manager who spoke first. "Ms. Harding, this is Henry Odin. He's here to visit with you."

Lena Harding pulled her glasses out of her pocket and put them on.

The manager added, "Ms. Harding, would you like for me to stay with you while he visits?"

Lena Harding shook her head and said, "No, I'll be okay."

"Ok then, I'll leave you two to your visit."

Lena Harding fixed her eyes on the coffee cup in her hand and then whispered in her weak voice, "What do you want, Henry?"

His voice grew shaky as he talked. "You know who I am?"

She nodded and then spoke, "The moment I saw the patch of blond hair on your head, I knew who you were."

Henry's eyes filled with tears. "Why didn't you say something the other day?"

She held her head up, looking far into the distance, and said, "What for? It's too late for anything. I'm dying, remember?"

A weakness rushed through his entire body, causing his heart to race.

"Henry, why did you come back today?"

He gazed at the duck bathing in the pond and then turned his attention back to Lena Harding, forming a blank look.

She signaled to him, "If you're not going to talk, maybe you should just leave."

He took a deep breath and sighed; "When I

saw you yesterday, I thought you resembled my mom. I felt like I needed to return to talk to you."

"Just leave the past alone Henry, what's done is done."

"All my life." His voice cracked, prompting him to cover his face until he regained his composure and then continued, "I wondered what had happened to you." Wiping his eyes he said, "And here you are, you've been alive all along, all these years."

Lena Harding kept quiet.

"Now I understand why I kept your memory alive in my heart all these years."

She finally responded, "Why?"

"Because my heart sensed you were alive out there somewhere and I just needed to find you."

Silence.

Henry continued, "Do you remember that day?"

Fearing Henry would discover the truth, Lena Harding pretended not to know what he was talking about when she said, "What day are you talking about, Henry?"

"It was the day you walked out the door and never returned. What happened to you that day? You told me you would be back in a few hours."

She knew the truth was on the verge of exposing itself, and yet she was determined to keep quiet. She simply said, "I don't know what you're talking about."

"You don't remember? You were rushing around, putting on a blue dress, the black shoes, and red stuff on your face."

Lena Harding closed her eyes and sighed heavily. A part of her had hoped to escape this moment, and yet the other part of her longed to have closure.

Henry continued, "I stood by the window and watched how a man escorted you into a red car. I cried out to you, but you ignored my cries. I was an eight-year-old kid. What were you thinking, leaving me alone like that and with nothing to eat?"

Lena Harding turned her wheelchair around so Henry couldn't see the emotional stress on her face. She couldn't hold the past in anymore. It was time to tell Henry the truth. She vented out, "I did return later that night. You were fast asleep on the sofa when I came in. I threw some clothes and things in a bag and walked right back out. Back then, my heart was in another place and I wasn't in a right frame of mind in those days. Pregnant at seventeen, I felt I was too young to be a mother. You were an obstacle that got in the way of my life. I wasn't ready to share my life, my money or anything else with some kid. I wanted my freedom."

Henry looked at her in disbelief. "You abandoned me?"

She turned her wheelchair back around to

face him and coldly replied. "Yes. I abandoned you."

At that moment, Henry's fear turned into anger. "All these years, I thought maybe something had happened to you. Never did I imagine you would disappear to keep from being a mother. Do you have any idea how hurtful it is to stand here and watch you tell me you never wanted me in your life?"

Lena Harding took a sip of her coffee and revealed, "And because of what I did, my life never amounted to anything." She removed her eyeglasses, wiped them clean on her garment. "When I left the apartment that night, I felt liberated, alive. Changed my name to Lena Harding and started a new life, thinking I was going to have the best life with no baggage hanging around. Then the accident happened and everything changed for me."

A thick silence fell between them until Henry found his voice again. "What accident?"

"An accident I had. I remember I could feel pain all over my body except my legs. I couldn't feel my legs. The doctor told me I would never walk again."

"How long ago did this happen?"

"I think it's been over twenty years, maybe longer. I don't remember anymore."

After hearing her story, Henry wanted to take the anger, the resentment and the bitterness he had packed away years back and bottle it up and throw it at her, but he couldn't. His heart wouldn't let him; instead his heart quietly gave way to compassion.

Lena Harding whispered, "My ignorance and my mistakes have made me a victim in all this too. You have no idea how I live with it every day. My past stares me in the face. It's inside, eating me alive. I can't escape it."

Henry shoved his hands in his pockets, lowered his head and closed his eyes, trying to find the right words to keep the conversation from getting heated.

"So what are you thinking, Henry? Go ahead, tell me."

"Tell you what?"

"Tell me I'm deserving of everything that's happened to me. That life is punishing me all these years for having abandoned you."

"I'm thinking about a verse in the Bible. It's somewhere in the book of Isaiah. It talks about a mother leaving behind her child, not having compassion for the child she carried in her womb."

"Are you making that up?"

"No, it goes on to say the mother forgot about her child, but God never did."

Lena's eyes became teary-eyed.

"Today, the world is full of stories like ours. Parents leading hurried lives feel pressured and tired that they become ignorant of a child's needs and wants, the abuse and the neglect set in. In our city, not one day goes by without hearing a child is mistreated or abandoned. It hurts to hear it."

"What are you trying to get at?" Lena asked.

Take a deep breath. Take a deep breath. Henry added, "If you had wanted me and given me a place in your heart when I was young, you and I would not be having this conversation right now. Our lives would be very different today."

"Oh, so now you're throwing it in my face?"

He took a moment to collect his thoughts and said, "No, I'm not. I don't want to bring more pain to you. What I'm trying to say is all I ever wanted from you was for you to love me and give me some kind of home, like all the other kids at school. That would have been enough."

Lena Harding held up her hand. "You need to stop."

I looked out at the grounds; the trees were displaying signs of fall. Odd looking shrubs along the fence were in the early stages of pretty fall colors too. I spotted songbirds flying above me. The beautifully manicured scene created the perfect moment to feel joy, to feel peace, something I longed to feel after finally finding my mother; instead, I felt a deep sadness not for myself but for her. She had robbed herself of love her entire life simply because of her un-willingness to make good choices in her younger years.

Lena Harding interrupted his thoughts, "So what became of your life, Henry?"

Startled by her question, he said, "What?"

"Tell me about your life. I want to know what happened to you after I left."

"It was rough for a while, but somewhere in there, God came in and saved me."

"So who raised you?" Lena asked.

After a lengthy stand, Henry took a seat on the bench underneath the tree. His palms were still sweating, "I went to live with grandma."

Lena Harding interrupted, "What grandma?"

Henry looked at Lena strangely. "Your mother. She didn't even know I existed. She was a sweet lady; so much compassion and love for everyone. She wore a crazy red scarf everywhere we went. Said it represented the blood of Jesus and it would protect her. In the evenings, she would sit in her rocking chair and tell me stories of the bible. Every night she would light a can-dle and pray for your return. She passed away shortly before I went off to college."

Lena Harding turned away, hoping Henry couldn't see the emotional stress on her face.

Henry gathered his courage and continued, "I want you to know, I spent my early childhood years looking out the window every chance I got, hoping one day you would return and take me in your arms, tell me, look I'm back, I love you, I'll never leave you again, but you never did." Henry's voice trailed off into a whisper.

She looked up at him. "I'm so sorry, Henry, for everything. If I could redo my life over, I would not have abandoned you. I would have figured out a way to care for you like I was suppose too."

Henry stood up from the bench and moved beside Lena's wheelchair. He studied her features. The wrinkly lines on her face were evidence of the hardships she had endured over the years. Her once beautiful green eyes were now faded, perhaps because of the pain and torment she'd endured over the years. And yet he still loved her.

He took a deep breath, sighed and then whispered to her, "I think God may have brought me here today, not so much for me but for you."

"Why do you say that?"

"God is aware of the shame you carry on the inside and he's seen the wrong choices you've made along the way. Sitting in this wheelchair for over twenty years, I think you've had a lot of time to think. Somewhere in there, your heart has undergone a change. And because of that change, God has already forgiven you."

"But never in my life have I stepped foot in a church. I'm nobody. How is God going to forgive me?"

"He does because he loves you."

By this time, the manager had returned to the door to see how Henry and his mother were getting along. Henry took note and regained his composure.

He said to Lena, "I think they may want you back inside. If it's okay with you, I would like to see you again. Maybe bring my family around to see you, too."

Her eyes teared up again. "No, it's okay. This visit you've made is enough."

By this time, Henry's anxiety had subsided. His heart finally felt at ease after finding his mom alive.

He continued, "Regardless of how life has turned out for us, you're still my mom and just as I loved you then, I love you now." He kissed her gently on the cheek.

She took his hand and held on to it tightly as she whispered, "Thank you."

Henry took hold of the wheelchair and said, "Let's take you back inside. I'm sure they are missing you by now."

He walked away, his heart feeling relieved not only for himself but also for his mother. Both had finally found the closure their hearts had been seeking for so long. Now he needed to go home and talk to Becca.

CHAPTER SIXTY-EIGHT

Henry returned home to find Becca in the dining room, papers scattered all over the table, her hair pinned in a messy bun. She had on the silly sweater dress he liked so much and those stupid cowboy boots.

He pulled a chair. "Making any sense of the stack?" He asked.

"Sort of. How's your heart?"

"I'm ok."

"Just ok?"

"It's a lot to process. Think I'm going to pull out my running shoes and go out to the trail. Need to think."

"Cleaned up Jonah's room and put on a set of clean sheets. Even added some pretty flowers. Just in case, you know."

He reached for her hand. "Have I told you I love you?"

She smiled, "Every day, all day."

I changed my clothing, grabbed my running shoes and stepped out into a mid day blue sky. The trail along my house was pretty deserted. Everyone was either at work or at school. Not that I didn't mind. But it made it much easier for me to stay focused in my head so I could hear my thoughts with no interruptions. Today, after almost thirty years of disappearing from my life, I found my mom at a facility not too far from my home. Some kind of accident twenty years earlier had left her paralyzed and strapped to a wheelchair. And now she was dying of cancer. Take a deep breath. Take a deep breath. A part of me wanted to feel angry after discovering she'd abandoned me in the middle of the night while I was asleep. The other part of me was relieved to have closure. And then there was my heart. There was no way my heart was going to abandon the love I'd been carrying around for her for so many years. Nor was I going to abandon her now that I had found her. So it was clear I had only one decision to make. I would move her in with my family.

CHAPTER SIXTY-NINE

Friday, December 6, 2013 (Few weeks later)

L ily ran into the room. "Grandpa, can I help?"
"I want to help too." Little Sara jumped
up and down.

Henry gathered Sara up in his arms. "Of
course you can help."

"Grandpa, why are we fixing this room? Is
Jonah coming back?" Lily asked.

Henry gently put Sara back down. "No, he's
all grown up now. My mom is coming to stay
with us."

"Grandpa, can we take her to church, too?"
Lily asked.

"Yes, and yes and yes. Girls come over here.
I have two small brushes and a tray. The paint
goes on the wall. Not on the floor, not on your
clothes and not on your faces. This paint is not
for face painting. Understood?"

They both nodded in unison.

Midway through the painting project, Lily
announced, "Grandpa, this is too much work."

Henry turned around to see his two girls

with smudges of paint on their clothes, their arms. He smiled. It was a memory moment for the family album. He helped them get cleaned up and off they went to play.

Hours later, Henry and Becca sat back and looked at each other. He spoke first. "What do you think?"

"I think the renovation looks great. We'll be able to fit a wheelchair through this door frame now with no problem. And the bathroom looks amazing."

"You think my mom will like it?"

"Oh gosh, yes, look around. What's not to like? This room is like the prettiest room in the house now."

He moved closer. "Are you jealous?"

She gave him a wet kiss. "Goodness, no, I have everything I need."

"You sure?"

She smiled, "Every day, all day."

He broke out laughing. "I love you."

"Oh yes, you do!" She whispered.

CHAPTER SEVENTY

Monday, December 9, 2013 (Few days later)

Henry looked at the clock. It was almost time. He was excited. He was scared. However, he knew this time everything would be ok, partly because Becca and the girls were in his life. But most importantly, because God was now present.

"It's going to be ok." Becca whispered.

Henry looked into his wife's blue eyes. They were filled with love, with compassion. It was precisely what he needed to get through this moment. He took her hand, whispered back, "I know."

The hospital van arrived at Henry's house by mid morning. Henry and Becca stood by the door, ready to welcome his mom. Henry wiped his teary eyes. Becca squeezed his hand tightly, indicating it was all going to be ok.

With her grey hair neatly styled back and wearing a pretty floral dress with matching slippers, a gift from Becca, Lena Harding held on to a small box on her lap as she was wheeled inside the home.

Henry was the first one to speak. "This is Becca, my wife."

Lena studied her features. "You're very pretty. You look like you have a good and tender heart."

Becca reached over and hugged her. "Henry and I are so happy you are here."

Lena's voice cracked. "Thank you."

Before the situation got mushy and teary eye again, Henry stepped in and said, "Mom, let me show you around. The house isn't too big. We adjusted some of the door frames for your wheelchair."

Lena looked around the home. "You have a nice house, Henry. You did good."

Take a deep breath. Take a deep breath. "Would you like to see your room now?" Henry asked.

Lena nodded.

The moment Henry wheeled her into her room; she became overwhelmed with emotion. "Henry, you did all this for me?" She asked.

"Yes mom. So you could have a nice room all to yourself. The nurse mentioned you like to watch television, so we put one in too."

Lena covered her face, crying she said, "Henry, I'm so sorry for the way I treated you."

Henry wiped his face, "No mom, we are not

looking back. We need to look forward to a new beginning in a new light. Even if it's for a little while."

"I love you." She whispered.

He had waited all his life to hear her tell him she loved him. He wanted to hold on to this moment forever.

Chapter Seventy-One

Wednesday, December 11, 2013 (Two days later)

Adjusting to having a new family member in the house would not come easy for the Odin family; nevertheless, they were all determined to make it work.

The caretaker arrived at precisely seven a.m. Then it was decided the therapist would come by at ten. By mid afternoon, the nurse had also paid a visit. And by late afternoon Lena Harding had all she could handle, forcing her to spend the rest of the afternoon in her room, hoping for some peace and quiet. Lily and Sara, however, had other plans. They burst into the room. Lena opened her eyes.

"Can we call you grandma?" Lily asked politely.

Lena gave her a weak smile, her tired voice whispered, "Yes you can."

"Do you like dolls?" Sara asked.

"I do."

"Can you play with us?" Lily asked.

"I don't have a doll." Lena replied.

Both girls ran out of the room, not but two minutes, and they were back with their collection of dolls, clothes, and other accessories.

"Grandma." Lily said. "Which doll do you want?"

"I like the one with the long dress. She looks like me."

"Ok grandma."

Sara was not to be left out. "Can I call you grandma too?"

"Of course you can."

Sara put her little arms around Lena; then asked her, "How come we never met you before?"

"Well, I was lost for a long time and couldn't find my way back."

"I'm happy grandpa found you." Lily said.

Thirty minutes later, Henry peeked his head into the room to see how everyone was getting along. It gave him pure joy to see his girls and his mom come together to enjoy a treasured moment. As much as he wanted to stand there and watch them continue with the doll playing, he needed to usher them into the kitchen to join Becca, who was busy with dinner preparations.

He entered the room. "Are you all having fun?"

Lena looked up at her son. "They wanted to play dolls." She said.

"How are you feeling?"

"Ok I guess."

"You feel like eating something?"

The caretaker, who had been in the room for most of the day, stepped in. "It will be time for her medication soon." She turned to Lena. "Ms. Harding, it might be good for you to eat something, or at least try."

Lena nodded her head.

Henry ushered the girls out of the room so the caretaker could adjust the wheelchair for Lena and take her to the dining room.

Henry came to Becca's rescue just as she was putting the finishing touches on her strawberry cream cheese cake minus the usual sugar. Today she had baked a special recipe so Lena could also enjoy some dessert.

Sara came around to Becca's side. "Mommy, is it my birthday?"

Both Henry and Becca smiled back at her. "No honey, not today." She said.

Lily chimed in, "Is it grandma's birthday?"

Henry replied, "No."

Lily continued, "Then why are we having cake?"

Henry added, "Because we want to celebrate having grandma here with us."

"Can she sit next to me?" Asked Lily.

"But what about me?" Asked Sara. "I want to sit next to grandma too."

And that's pretty much how the dinner conversation played out in the Odin household for the good part of the evening. Henry would have it no other way. His dreams were becoming reality, all thanks to the kindness he had shown his mother, despite their past.

CHAPTER SEVENTY-TWO

Wednesday, December 25, 2013
(Christmas Day)

L ily was the first to wake up, followed by Sara. Both made their way to the Christmas tree as fast as they could. And as soon as Henry heard their pattering feet, he and Becca were on their way, too. Shortly thereafter, the caretaker wheeled Lena out to the living room. It was the first time she'd seen a family gather around a Christmas tree, almost like children at a candy store. She became teary eye recalling memories of how Henry always begged her for toys, for shoes, for clothes. And she would always ignore his cries.

Henry noticed her somber look. "You ok mom?"

"I'm good." She whispered.

"We are waiting for Alvin and Jeanie to get here so we can open presents."

She nodded, went back to fixing her pretty pink dress.

Minutes later, Jonah arrived with his girlfriend. Not too long after that, Alvin and Jeanie Beard walked through the front door, arms filled with trays of goodies. They enlisted Henry and Jonah to bring in the presents. Lily and Sara could hardly contain their excitement.

"Grandpa, when can we open our presents?" Lily asked Henry.

"How about if you and Sara go sit next to the tree? I think Becca wants us to take a picture first."

"But that's too much time." Sara replied.

Henry tickled them silly and sent them back to the Christmas tree where everyone else was already in place, including Lena.

Once the caretaker snapped the family photos, they all disbursed to different areas of the living room. It was Lily and Sara who opened their gifts first. Lena sat back in her wheelchair, quietly observing as the family came together in spirit and in love to share the most important day of the year, prompting her to recall when Henry was young and how she never celebrated the holidays or birthdays with him. In those days, she was so wrapped up in her world; she had no idea the child needed love or attention.

"Mom, this one is for you." Henry handed Lena a present.

Lena looked up at him, her eyes teary. "For me?" She asked.

"Yeah, you're part of the family. Go ahead, open it up."

Lena pulled the bow off and tore the wrapping apart to find a neatly folded red scarf.

Henry sat next to her and said, "It was grandma's. I thought you might want to have it."

She broke out crying, "Thank you."

Henry reached over and hugged her. "Don't cry. Then I start crying too."

Now it was Becca's turn to give Henry his present. She came over to the sofa and squeezed herself between Henry and the girls, who were busy with their new dolls.

Henry looked at his wife. She had the most beautiful, serene look on her face. He couldn't resist; he kissed her on the cheek.

She said, "Go ahead, and open it."

He pulled the red string, opened the small box to find a key. He looked at Becca, somewhat puzzled, and then asked, "And the key is for what? Are we having another baby?"

She laughed, "No silly." She glanced over at her dad and mom and then back at Henry and said, "Dad is giving you his red convertible. The car is in great condition. I know you've always liked it."

Henry glanced over at Alvin and Jeanie. "Thank you so much, but..."

"No but, it's yours. I don't have any use for it anymore." Alvin said.

Henry looked at Becca. "Maybe we can take it for a ride later."

Becca gave him a quick peck on the cheek and then turned to everyone. "So, who wants breakfast?"

"Mommy I want pancakes." Sara's small voice said.

"And I want sausages." Lily chimed in.

"And I will help." Added Henry.

Lena watched from a distance as her son made his way to the kitchen, instantly blending in with his family. It surprised her to see him cook side by side with his wife and his girls. Looking back, she came to realize she never took the time to cook or do anything in the kitchen other than store her cold beverages. How Henry must have starved. She closed her eyes, trying to forget her nasty past.

Before long, everyone had made their way to the dining room, where breakfast would be served. Lena was seated at one end of the table with the two girls side by side. Jonah and his girlfriend sat across from Alvin and Jeanie while Henry and Becca were seated at the opposite end. All started well with the delicious breakfast, small talk around the table, and the infectious laughter until someone decided to ask Lena about her accident.

That someone was Alvin. "Lena, if you don't mind me asking, how did you end up in the wheelchair? Henry says you had an accident."

Lena dropped her fork, looked up with a hazy look in her eyes.

Henry sensed her sudden change in mood. "You ok mom?"

Lena put up her hand to keep Henry from going any further. She spoke in her weak voice. "It was my wedding day. I had finally found a man who was interested in me for me. Even after all I had done and been through. I had been planning my wedding for months. It was going to be my first time getting married. I envisioned a beautiful home with this man. Maybe start fresh and have more kids. That day, I was running late. I had forgotten to pick up the wedding rings, so I decided I would put on my wedding dress, fix up my hair, makeup and leave early to get the wedding rings and then head over to the club. We were going to get married at the club where we had met. I was on the road, coming up on an intersection; my light was green, out of nowhere a car makes a turn in front of my lane, I couldn't stop. I don't remember much after that. I guess it was a day or two after the accident when I woke up in a hospital. My body was hurting all over except my legs. I couldn't feel my legs. The doctor came in to talk to me. At first, I didn't really understand what he was trying to tell me. A few days later, he talked to me again. It was then that I came too and realized I would never walk again. The man I was going to marry came to see me at the hospital. When he found out I'd been paralyzed from the waist down, he told me he couldn't take care of me. He told me this wasn't supposed to happen. He blamed me for the entire incident. So he left. I never saw him again." Lena wiped her eyes.

"I'm so sorry to hear that." Alvin then asked, When did your accident happen?"

"I remember it as if it were yesterday, February 6, 1981."

Alvin and Jeanie looked at each other.

Henry drew his eyebrows in. Take a deep breath. Take a deep breath.

Becca lowered her head and stared down at her plate.

The silence was so thick; you could almost hear a heartbeat.

It was Alvin who took the initiative to speak first. His voice emotional. "We lost our son Tony years ago. Think it was about the same time." He looked directly at Lena and asked her, "Do you remember anything about the car that crossed your path?"

Lena's voice was growing tired by now, but she continued anyway. "I remember the doctor telling me there were three people in the car. A kid in the back seat had died."

The room fell silent again. Jeanie gripped Alvin's arm. With no further conversation on the matter, everyone realized at the table Lena Harding had been the driver behind the wheel who struck the Beard vehicle on February 6, 1981, killing thirteen-year-old Tony Beard, Henry's childhood friend who lived across the street.

What was supposed to have been said in response to the revelation would never be known because on that day the Beard family, as much as Henry, chose to let go of the past and forgive, thanks to their tender hearts.

Henry looked around the room, taking notice of the somber feeling hanging over like a grey cloud. They all knew he had spent a lifetime searching, waiting to see his mother again. Why create any discord, knowing she was already dying of cancer, anyway? And if they did, he might very well lose her much sooner than later.

He took a deep breath and spoke; "I think we need to push through our breakfast so we can make church at noon. It's tough to find parking on a day like today."

CHAPTER SEVENTY-THREE

Wednesday, December 25, 2013
(Christmas Day - hours later)

Henry wheeled Lena Harding into the church. Trailing behind was the rest of the family. For the first time in his life, he was going to have the opportunity to experience the spirit of Christmas with his mother by his side, along with his family. He quietly took his seat next to her while Becca sat on the other side of him. Next to each other were the two girls with the Beard family sitting at the far end of the wooden bench. For most of the service, Lena Harding kept quiet and to herself. She held her hands in her lap. At one point Henry asked her if she was ok. She simply nodded. It was perhaps a sign she had found the peace she needed in her heart to finally let go.

And after all Henry had been through and endured over the years, he too was ready to finally find some peace in his heart and put the past behind him and look to the future with his family.

Several hours later and into the evening, Lena Harding was rushed to a nearby hospital where she passed away in the presence of her son, Henry Odin. He couldn't believe it. Having found her after a lifetime of searching and, just like that, he had lost her again. This time, it was forever. He buried his cries in his hands.

Chapter Seventy-Four

Friday, April 18, 2014
(Almost four months later)

Henry kept his eye on the clock as he sipped the last of his coffee. He rubbed his chin. Whispering, he said, "Going to be late again." Pulling on his boots when he heard Becca's car in the driveway. She was returning from dropping the girls off at school. She walked through the door to find Henry lacing his boots. By his side was his favorite baseball cap, which she secretly loved but had never mentioned it.

"What are you doing?" She whispered.

"Just getting ready to go check on a job."

"Can you play hooky today? It's Friday."

He looked up at his wife; she certainly knew how to stir up his heart. Hair pulled back in a messy ponytail. An oversized white shirt, cutoff shorts and those stupid cowboy boots.

"What did you have mind?" He asked.

"How about if we take a drive to see the country roads? The spring flowers are out."

He wasn't going to pass up alone time with his wife.

"I'll pull the car out while you change." She said.

He smiled. "What's wrong with the way I look?"

"It's not romantic enough."

He laughed, "Does it matter?"

"Today it does." She said.

"Have I told you I love you?"

"Every day, all day."

CPSIA information can be obtained
at www.ICGtesting.com
Printed in the USA
BVHW080821030123
655382BV00003B/276